The Temporary Gentleman

SEBASTIAN BARRY

PENGUIN BOOKS

PENGUIN BOOKS

Published by the Penguin Group
Penguin Group (USA) LLC
375 Hudson Street
New York, New York 10014

USA | Canada | UK | Ireland | Australia | New Zealand | India | South Africa | China
penguin.com
A Penguin Random House Company

First published in Great Britain by Faber and Faber Limited, 2014
First published in the United States of America by Viking Penguin,
a member of Penguin Group (USA) LLC, 2014
Published in Penguin Books 2015

THE LIBRARY OF CONGRESS HAS CATALOGED THE
HARDCOVER EDITION AS FOLLOWS:
Barry, Sebastian, 1955–
The temporary gentleman / Sebastian Barry.
pages cm
ISBN 978-0-670-02587-9 (hc.)
ISBN 978-0-14-312712-3 (pbk.)
1. Irish—Ghana—Fiction. 2. World War, 1939–1945—Veterans—
Fiction. 3. United Nations—Officials and employees—Fiction. 4. Married
people—Fiction. 5. Man-woman relationships—Fiction. I. Title.
PR6052.A729T47 2014
823'.914—dc23
2013047831

Printed in the United States of America
1 3 5 7 9 10 8 6 4 2

Praise for Sebastian Barry

"Barry, the greatest prose writer in Irish letters—which by definition makes him the greatest writer of prose in the English language. . . . No other novelist now writing can convey as Barry does the way in which unrighted wrongs continue to reverberate down through the ages, creating new versions of old tragedies for people with no knowledge of their origins."   —Allen Barra, *The Daily Beast*

"Sebastian Barry's handling of voice and cadence is masterly. His fictional universe is filled with life, quiet truth, and exquisite intimacy; it is also fully alert to the power and irony of history."
—Colm Tóibín, author of the Costa Novel Award–winning *Brooklyn*

"Language of surpassing beauty . . . It is like a song, with all the pulse of the Irish language."   —*The New York Times*

"Barry succeeds admirably in creating complex individuals who find themselves trapped in a brutal reality."   —*Los Angeles Times*

"Prose of often startling beauty."
          —Margot Livesey, author of *The Flight of Gemma Hardy*

"Luminous and lyrical."   —*O, The Oprah Magazine*

"Barry is extravagantly talented."   —*Chicago Tribune*

"[Barry's] words have a stony allure of the Irish poets and the lyrical pull of an epic storyteller."   —*The Boston Globe*

"Sebastian Barry makes the fine distinction between sentiment and sentimentality with a deft hand. . . . The sheer liveliness of Barry's writing, his sure handling of the wide variety of characters and their dialogue, and the resilient Lilly herself all ensure that the novel doesn't bog down in her sorrows."   —*The Philadelphia Inquirer*

"Tripping, liquid prose that adroitly evokes everything from the smell of an Irish countryside to the heaviness of grief."   —*Booklist*

ABOUT THE AUTHOR

Sebastian Barry has won the Costa Book of the Year Award, the Hughes & Hughes Irish Novel of the Year Award, the James Tait Black Memorial Prize, and the Walter Scott Prize. His work has twice been short-listed for the Man Booker Prize. He is the author of five previous novels and lives in Ireland.

To access Penguin Readers Guides online, visit our Web site at www.penguin.com.

To Jacquie Burgess,
beautiful and wise

Hic amor, haec patria est.

VIRGIL, *AENEID*

Remember me, forget my fate.

NAHUM TATE, DIDO AND AENEAS

Chapter One

'It's a beautiful night and no mistake. You would never think there was a war somewhere.'

These less than prophetic words were spoken by a young navy second lieutenant, on the wide, night-bedarkened deck of our supply ship, bound for Accra. He was a tubby little man, whom the day's sun had scorched red. Happy to hear an Irish accent I asked him where he was from and he said, with that special enthusiasm Irish people reserve for each other when they accidentally meet abroad, Donegal. We talked then about Bundoran in the summer, where my father had often brought his band. It was a pleasure to shoot the breeze with him for a few moments as the engines growled on, deep below.

The cargo was eight hundred men and officers, all headed for various parts of British Africa. There was the noise of the little parliaments of the card-players, and the impromptu music-halls of the whisky drinkers, and true enough a lovely mole-grey air moved across the ship in a beneficent wave. We could see the coast of Africa lying out along a minutely fidgeting shoreline. The only illuminations were the merry lights of the ship, and the sombre philosophical lights of God above. Otherwise the land ahead was favoured only by darkness, a confident brushstroke of rich, black ink.

I had been in an excellent mood for days, having picked the winner of the Middle Park Stakes at Nottingham. Every so often, I stuck a hand in my right pocket and jingled part of my winnings in the shape of a few half-crowns. The rest of it was inserted into an inside pocket of my uniform – a fold of lovely crisp white banknotes. I'd got up to Nottingham on a brief furlough, having been given a length of time not quite long enough to justify the long trek across England and Ireland to Sligo.

France had fallen to Hitler, and suddenly, bizarrely, colonies like the Gold Coast were surrounded by the new enemy, the forces of the Vichy French. No one knew what was going to happen, but we were being shunted down quickly to be in place to blow bridges, burst canals, and break up roads, if the need arose. We had heard the colonial regiments were being swelled by new recruits, thousands of Gold Coast men rushing to defend the Empire. I suppose this was when Tom Quaye, though of course I didn't know him then, joined up.

So I was standing there, flush with my winnings, not thinking of much, as always somewhat intoxicated by being at sea, somewhat in love with an unknown coastline, and the intriguing country lying in behind. I had also about a bottle of Scotch whisky in me, though I stood rooted as a tree for all that. It was a moment of simple exhilaration. My red hair, the selfsame red hair that had first brought me to the attention of Mai, for it was not I who said hello to her first, but she, with her playful question in the simple neat quadrangle of the university, 'I suppose you put a colour in that?' – my red hair was brushed flat back from my forehead, my second licutenant's cap holding it down like a pot lid, my cheeks had been shaved by my batman Percy Welsh, my under-clothes were starched, my trousers were creased, my shoes were signalling back brightly to the moon – when suddenly the whole port side of the ship seemed to go up, right in front of my eyes, an enormous gush and gey-ser of water, a shuddering explosion, an ear-numbing rip of metallic noise, and a vast red cornet of flames the size of the torch on the Statue of Liberty. The young second lieutenant from Donegal was suddenly as dead as one of those porpoises you will see washed up on the beach at Enniscrone after a storm, on the deck beside me, felled by a jagged missile of stray metal. Men came tearing up from below, the doorways oozing them out as if so much boiling molasses, there were cries and questions even as the gigantic fountain of displaced water col-lapsed and found the deck, and hammered us flat there as if we were blobs of dough. Two of my sappers were trying to peel me back up from the deck, itself splintered and cratered from the force, and now other stray bits of the ship rained down, clattering and banging and boasting and killing.

'That was a fucking torpedo,' said my sergeant, with perfect redundancy, a little man called Ned Johns from Cornwall, the most knowledgeable man for a fuze I ever worked with. He probably knew the make and poundage of the torpedo, but if he did he didn't say. The next second the huge ship started to pitch to port, and before I could grab him, Ned Johns went off sliding down the new slope and smashing into the rail, gathered himself, stood up, looked back at me, and then was wrenched across the rail and out of view. I knew we were holed deep under the waterline, I could more or less feel it in my body, something vital torn out of the ship echoed in the pit of my stomach, some mischief done, deep, deep in some engine room or cargo hold.

My other helper, Johnny 'Fats' Talbott, a man so lean you could have used him for spare wire, as poor Ned Johns once said, in truth was using me now as a kind of bollard, but that was no good, because the ship seemed to make a delayed reaction to its wound, and shuddered upward, the ship's rail rearing up ten feet in a bizarre and impossible movement, catching poor Johnny completely off guard, since he had been bracing himself against a force from the other direction, and off he went behind me, pulling the trouser leg off my uniform as he did so, sending my precious half-crowns firing in every direction.

So for a moment of odd calm I stood there, one leg bare to the world, my cap still in place inexplicably, myself drenched so thoroughly I felt one hundred per cent seawater. An iron ladder full of men, from God knows where, maybe even from inside the ship, or from the side of the command deck more likely, with about a dozen calling and screaming persons clinging to it like forest monkeys, moved past me as if it were a trolley being wheeled by the demon of this attack, and crossed the ravaged deck, and pitched down into the moiling, dark sea behind. Everything roared for that moment, the high night sky of blankening stars, the great and immaculate silver serving dish of the sea itself, the rended ship, the offended and ruined men – and then, precipitatively, a silence reigned, the shortest reign of any silence in the empires of silence, the whole vista, the far-off coast, the deck, the sea, was as still for a moment as a painting, as if someone had just painted it all in his studio, and was gazing at it, contemplating it, reaching out to put a finishing touch on it, of smoke, of fire, of blood, of water, and then I felt the whole ship leave me, sink under my boots so suddenly that there was for that second a gap between me and it, so that wasn't I like an angel, a winged man suspended. Then gravity broke the spell, gravity ruined the bloody illusion, and I went miserably and roaringly downward with the ship, the deck broke into the waters, it smashed through the sacred waters like a child breaks an ice puddle in a Sligo winter, it made a noise like that, of something solid, something icy breaking, glass really, but not glass, infinitely soft and receiving water, the deeps, the dreaded deeps, the reason why fishermen never learn to swim, let the waters take us quickly, let there be no thrashing and hoping and swimming, no, let your limbs go, be calm, put your trust in God, pray quick to your Redeemer, and I did, just like an Aran fisherman, and gave up my soul to God, and sent my last signal of love flying back across Europe to Mai, Mai, and my children, up the night-filthied coast of Africa, across the Canaries, across the old boot of England and the ancient baby-shape of Ireland, I sent her my last word of love, I love thee, I love thee, Mai, I am sorry, I am sorry.

The ocean closed over my head with its iron will, and the fantastical suck of the sinking ship drew me down as if a hundred demons were yanking on my legs, down down we went, our handsome troopship made in Belfast, the loose bodies of the already drowned, the myriad papers and plans for war, the tins of sardines we had taken in in Algiers, the fabulous materiel, the brand new trucks, the stocks of tyres, the fifty-three horses, the wooden stakes, the planks, the boxes of carefully stored explosives, all down down to Neptune we went, extinguished in a moment without either glory or cowardice, an action of the gods, of queer physics, that huge metal mass sucker-punched, beaten, ruined, wrecked, fucked to all hell as Ned Johns would say, and I felt the water all around as if I were in the body of a physical creature, as if this were its blood, and the scientifically explainable forces at work were its sinews and muscles. And it stopped my mouth and found the secret worm-whorls of my ears, and it wanted entry into me, but I had grabbed, stolen, fetched out with an instinctive exuberance, a last great gulp of breath, and I was bearing this down with me, in my chest, around my heart, as my singing response, my ears were now thundering with the thunders of the sea, I thought I could hear the ship itself cry out in a crazy vocabulary of pain, as if a man could learn this lingo somewhere, the tearing death-cries of a vessel. All the while as if still standing on the deck, but that was not possible, and then I thought the ship was turning sideways, like a giant in its bed, and I had no choice but to go with it, I was like a salmon looking for the seam in a waterfall, where it could grip its way to the gravel-beds on grips of mere water, and now I thought I was rushing over the side, away from the deck, accelerated by some unknown force faster than the ship itself, and I was scraping along metal, I felt long sea-grass and barnacles, surely I could not have, but I thought I did, and just as the ship went right over, or so I imagined it, how could I know, in the deepest dark, the darkest deepest dark that ever was, an instance of utter blankness, suddenly I felt the very keel of the troopship, something wide and round and good, the sacred keel, the foundation of the sailor's hope, the guarantor of his sleep between watches, but all up the wrong way, in the wrong place, violently torn from its proper place, and just in that moment, just in that moment, with a great groan, a weird and menacing sighing, a sort of silence as the worst noise in creation, the keel halted and went back the other way, like the spine of a whale, as if the ship were now fish, and because I was holding onto the keel, riding it, like a fly on a saddle, it sort of threw me back the other way, catapulted me slowly, Mr Cannonball himself in the tuppenny circus of old at Enniscrone, my childhood flaring in my head, my whole life flaring, and then I seemed to be in the shrouds of the little forward mast, and I squeezed my body into a tight ball, again pure instinct, not a thought in my mind, and as the killed ship rolled slowly over, seeking its doom at least in a balletic and beautiful curve, the furled sails rolled me over and over, giving me strange speed, volition unknown, and I unfolded myself, like a lover rising victorious from the marriage bed, and I spread my arms, and I thrashed them into the ocean, and swam, and swam, looking for the surface, praying for it, gone a mile beyond mere breathlessness, ready to grow gills to survive this, and then it was there, the utterly simple sky, God's bare lights, in the serene harbours of the constellations, and I grabbed like a greedy child onto something, a shard of something, a ruined and precious fragment, and there I floated, gripping on, half-mad, for a minute without memory, oh Mai, Mai, for a minute all absence and presence, a creature blanked out and destroyed, a creature bizarrely renewed.

By the grace of God we were travelling in convoy that night. And by the grace of God, for some reason only known to its captain and its crouching sailors, the submarine melted off into the deeps, not that any of us saw it. A corvette bristling with machine guns manoeuvered up near me, I heard the confident voices with wild gratitude, arms reached down into the darkness for me, pulled me from the chaos, and I slumped, suddenly lumpish and exhausted, at the boots of my rescuers, falling down to lie with other survivors, some with dark-blooded wounds, a few entirely naked, the clothes sucked off them.

I lay there, ticking with life, triumphant, terrified. I noticed myself checking my inside pocket for the roll of banknotes, as if watching someone else, as if I were two people, and I laughed at my other self for his foolishness.

We steamed into Accra the following morning.

Chapter Two

Now it is 1957 and I am back in Accra, after many comings and goings. The war has been over for twelve years. The Gold Coast has turned into Ghana, the first African country to gain independence. As a former UN observer I watched it all with immense interest and excitement – the enormous politeness of the departing British, the beautiful speeches, the Ciceronian phrases. We are very good at leaving. At the same time, there is still a governor here for the moment, and a skeleton of the old administration. There are currents of darkness in this bright new river and slowly-slowly seems to be the ticket, for fear of old hatreds and old scores fomenting up – indeed as they did in Ireland in the twenties.

Soon I'll go back to Sligo. It is so strange to be in a freed country, and yet not so strange, since my own home place once was freed. I did not understand freedom. I understand it better now, just a little. I have been renting this little plaster house, with an old design of swirls and squares on the outside, like one of the local temples. It is not a temple, but the temperate, honest quarters of a minor official, Mr Peter Oko, who was happy to rent out his extra house to this whiteman, while gainfully employed by the UN, and now staying on when many of his type, 'the others' who have haunted Africa for three hundred years, have packed their trunks and gone. When I first arrived over a year ago he was described to me by the lady, whose name I forget, in the letter from the UN, as 'the lovely Mr Oko, who will help you in all things'. And he was as good as her word. Two thirds my height, with a penny-sized patch of baldness on his pleasant crown, fluent in English, more so than many an Irishman, he kept me fully informed and decently housed throughout the period of my contract. Maybe a few years my senior, he referred to me as 'his son', as in, 'Mr McNulty, my son,' and generally gave himself and all his fellow Accrans a good name in my heart. And I remember Accra when it was all tin roofs and ant hills, long before the war, and it was the despair of the European wives, asking the old administrative headquarters here by means of persistent and frantic letters for information about dresses, hats, and most urgently of all, mosquito-proof stockings, as we lurked vulnerably in our distant station.

The local English newspaper, the *Accran Clarion*, whose pages have shrunk from twenty to one single sheet, says there is still a little trouble here and there, that old trouble for instance bubbling back up between Togoland and the Gold Coast that I and others laboured to fix just a few months ago. If the men come in their new uniforms to ask me to quit their Ghana, of course I will have to go. But as yet nothing disturbs the delightful atmosphere here at the edge of the city, where the houses give way to the bright green squares of passionately growing vegetables. I cannot see the Atlantic, but I can smell it, half a mile distant, that hazy and infinite expanse of acres, with its immense depths, and sometimes terrifying waters. So I am content enough not to be in sight of it. Even as I looked it over last year, the house I mean, with Mr Oko, and he darted about showing me its glories and idiosyncrasies, I was thinking, 'But Mai would have liked to be by the sea, for the swimming.' And with the next thought remembered she would not be living here with me.

Mai.

And I will go back to Ireland, I must, I must, I have duties there, not least to my children.

❧

1922. There she was, the first time I ever saw her, sailing along in her loose black skirts, her lovely face above a long-boned frame, on the cinder path of the university, hidden by tree trunks and then revealed, so that she whirred in my eyes like a film reel, a shadow half-ruined by sunlight under the famous plane trees. Her blouse so white, with the soft bosom plainly moving within, that it was a bright shield in the underwood. And myself still very young, when the brain seemed to brook no real thought of the past or the future – the movement of time and the world stilled. I watched her from under the dark arch of the entrance to the quadrangle. It was still my first year in the university, in the time of the civil war.

She had many friends, chief of them a splendid girl called Queenie Moran, a great favourite in the college, but none of them among my own set, which was very male I suppose, technical-minded boys among the engineers, and those dark, mysterious chaps who got light only from the more distant galaxies of mathematics and physics. Her friends were the new girls of the century, who had come into the university on fearless feet, and who swished up and down the paths of the college with the confidence of Cortez and Magellan. Sometimes she could be seen in the small swarm of these women, coming out of lectures talking fast and loud, well aware I do not doubt of the lonesome male gazes thrown their way. And then there were those boys in their set that can insert themselves among a group of women, a talent in itself, the sons of doctors and even people in the new government, with the smoke of both victory and surrender drifting above their heads.

The way I found out she lived on the Grattan Road was I followed her home one evening, keeping at a distance behind her, like a detective or a thief, as she swept along the seafront. I was impressed by the fact that she never looked back, not once. The glass-dark acreage of the bay over to her left and the muddle of small cottages and bigger houses to her right seemed to funnel her efficiently all the way to Salthill.

She disappeared in through old gate-posts with granite balls on top. I knew there must be metal spikes securing them invisibly and I found myself hoping her father did not have a similar spike in him, for the place spoke of considerable status and grandeur. I watched her open the big front door, go in, drag off her hat and scarlet coat and, with her right boot raised behind her like a skater, without looking back out into the dreary evening, kick the door shut.

In order for her to make her first remark to me, I had to keep putting myself in her way. I didn't know any other method to utilise. I placed myself near her as she wandered out of one of her commerce lectures. I had watched her go in, spent the hour of the lecture traipsing about – and then more or less threw myself in her path. Terrified but resolute.

'I suppose you put a colour in that?' she said, looking at my red hair. 'Who are you anyway? Everywhere I go, you seem to pop up like a Jack-in-the-box.'

'Well, my name *is* Jack, now you mention it.'

'Which of the Jacks are you?' she said, as if there were a hundred Jacks in her life.

'Jack McNulty,' I said. 'John Charles McNulty.' Then I added, as if for full illumination: 'Engineering.'

She was silent for a moment. What I noticed suddenly was that she was nervous too, I am not quite sure how I knew that, but I did. Of course she was nervous, she was only nineteen years old, accosted by a blushing, red-haired boy she had never met.

'That's a decent handle. I'm Mai Kirwan,' she said, as if anyone would be fully aware of the name, and she was now but putting a face to it.

Then, as if we were diplomats at a border somewhere, she held out her gloved hand. The glove was an orange-coloured leather. I stared at the hand a moment, then rushed to shake it lightly. She smiled at me and laughed.

'No doubt I'll see you about the place,' she said, maybe not having the arsenal of phrases to bring us any further.

'You will,' I said, 'you will,' and then she was past me in a pleasant fog of perfume, and gone.

That was how it started.

✺

It is evening now in the fringy fields. Tom Quaye was here all day, and cooked a lovely fish stew with okra and palm-nut. He sings songs in Ewe under his breath the whole time, and has excellent English from an Irish priest who taught him years ago. Indeed he has a bit of a Roscommon accent, which makes me homesick. It was Mr Oko found Tom. He is the perfect houseboy for me, as he was in the Gold Coast Regiment in the war. He survived the horrors of Burma, and finished up a sergeant major. He is a big, wide man that scorns shoes, and indeed as far as I remember NCOs of the GCR didn't always wear shoes, even on parade. He is exactly my age, down to the very month, as I noted from his scrupulous papers.

There was some trouble with pensions when he came home from the war and he and his fellows marched in protest through Accra, and the police killed some of them. Which was a poor way to say thank you for their defence of the Empire, no doubt. But he doesn't say too much about this, and is more concerned to fashion a decent stew, or whatever he happens to be doing. Sweeping out the ants. Shining up the whisky glasses. He just gets on with it. Life. Precious life.

I pay him two shillings a day, which is a bob less than Eneas got in the Royal Irish Constabulary in the twenties, at home in Ireland, which was his undoing. 'The ould death sentence' as Eneas quaintly called it, conferred on him by his own childhood butty, Jonno Lynch, in best Irish style. Now Eneas is in exile somewhere and I don't know where he is. Easy money is a treacherous thing.

In the army, Tom tells me, he was paid a bob a day, unlike most of the other nationalities, who got two. They kept a third back from his pay too, which was to be given to him as a sort of bonus after the war. This came to £23 in his case, for three years' fighting, including Burma. As for a pension, he says only wounded lads get one of those, and it's only a pittance really. Thousands of soldiers couldn't find work, and they all pledged themselves to Nkrumah as a result. The best you could hope for was a job in the police, but Tom didn't want to do that, especially after being shot at by the same gentlemen. He says he was a happy man when Mr Oko sent him a message that there was a sort of job going with me, although I am not sure he really knows how short-lived it might be. It sufficeth for the day, I suppose.

Tom has a wife and children upcountry somewhere that he never sees. Up along the Volta river somewhere, he did say the name of the village, but I didn't retain it. The reason for this is apparently that the wife won't let him come. He told me that regularly he sends a message to her, asking if he can see his sons and daughters. The messenger has to take a bus, walk twenty miles, and then hire two boats. It is very expensive for Tom. But she always sends a message back to say no. It was strange when he talked about this to see his usually confident, 'manly' face in disarray.

It took him a few months to confide in me. I had asked him to sit but he didn't sit, he just stood there, telling me about his wife.

'Some day I pray she will tell me to come,' he said.

———

On my new writing table – which I bought in the laby-
rinthine Kingsway department store in Accra, breasting
my way through the great sea of wives – is an old photo
of myself, in a flyblown frame. A chubby six-year-old
child on Strandhill beach with a wooden spade and one
of those wintry smiles that little boys specialise in. I am
holding up the spade with pride to the person taking the
photograph. My father, with his box Brownie. When I
look at the photo of course I can see myself, but I can
also still see him, standing on the sand in his black suit,
frowning down at the viewer, and yet smiling, being a
somewhat contradictory person sometimes, like a sun-
shower.

When we were small boys, myself, Eneas, and Tom –
Teasy came later – my father used to come in at night
and make himself what he called 'the great bird'. He
would stand at our bedsides and spread his arms, and
we would try to disappear under the blankets, the three
of us in a row in the single bed. With our eyes closed,
half terrified, half crazy with delight, we would sense
'the great bird' slowly slowly alighting above us, and
then we would feel the human kiss he laid on each of
our foreheads.

When I was ten I asked him not to be the great bird
any more, and watched his face alter with emotion as
he agreed. The difficulty was, he couldn't reach the

part of the kiss without it, so myself, Tom, and Eneas went without.

My mother, small, black-clothed as if she were already a widow, was the foundation stone that I based my stability on, like the pier of a bridge. If she seemed harsh sometimes when I was small, it was only a habit that had got a hold of her. And there were times, in particular when my father was away in Roscommon or Mayo with his little orchestra, when she was inclined to take your arm, and tell you things, funny, quick and startling things, little truths, stories maybe of her youth, before her marriage. And she would stand on the hearthstone of the tiny parlour, and show us one of her dances, which she performed with great dexterity and expertise. And her children would stare gobsmacked at her as she clattered her soles on the black slate.

She rarely addressed my father directly, but called him 'he' and 'him' – even when he was in the old doss beside her. It was a curious habit.

Her occasional crossness had its roots in her terror of being connected to a mystery, something clouded, which was the unknown story of her true origin. She had been raised by the Donnellans, but had eventually found out she was not theirs. This tore at my mother's core. My mother had a horror of her own self sometimes, and her great fear, and the word fear does not encompass her suffering, was that she was illegitimate, which then and now can make a small pit of torment inside a person's soul. Not that she ever spoke of this to me, even when I was a young man, it was Pappy told me about it, in familial whispers.

My father for his part loved nothing more than going out on those sorties with his band. All kitted out in his best suit, his straw boater cocked sideways, he would shove his instruments into the pony and trap, and often me also. I was reckoned to be a decent hand at shaving a reed, or replacing a string. Not to lower the high tone of the band I was also kitted out in a little frock coat perfectly sewn by him, down to the tiny tin buttons.

But my father was also the tailor in the Sligo Lunatic Asylum, that was his real job.

Every year the staff there held their dance, clearing the lunatics back into the further recesses of the enormous building and dragging the old benches out of the Lunatics' Hall. So then I was standing at the rear of an impromptu platform with my penknife poised and my spare strings. I had a privileged view of the buoyant arses of the band, and their bobbing boaters. They wiggled and twisted their bodies like seaweed in the sea as they ground out the evening's music, and the little crowd of revellers milled in a democratic maelstrom on the huge drum of the floorboards. There was something of mania in the wildness of it, as if only mania after all could be manifested in an asylum. Arms were flung around like hurlers, legs were swung in extravagant moves. Normally sober and discouraged females were nearly thrown into the air during the set dances. And I stood there, my face open and staring, delighted with everything, while my father lashed away on the violin, or drove at the cello with his stick like he was trying to saw himself in half.

Then in the little back room, when all was done, and the motley dancers had drifted home, we would eat big white sandwiches, the jam a bloodstain on the bread, and drink cold, cold glasses of milk, the only music now the drifting cries and lamentations of the inmates, raging or sorrowing in the rooms of the echoing building.

Standing beside the little photo of myself, a genuine relic now, is a daguerreotype of my great-uncle Thomas McNulty, who was scalped by a band of Comanches in the central grasslands of Texas. He was a trooper in the US cavalry. It is so faded that I can only just make him out, in his blue uniform. My father was named after him, and my brother too, necessitating the terms Old Tom and Young Tom. It was this photograph made me want to be a soldier when I was small.

It was our bit of 'ancestry', a thing thin on the ground in general in my family. My father also told me with great solemnity that we had once been butter exporters in Sligo, and had lived in a mansion called the Lungey House, just around the corner from our quarters on John Street. This old place was by then a charmless and festering ruin. In an even more heartfelt confidence, he told me that up to the time of Cromwell, our ancestor, Oliver McNulty, had been chief of his tribe, only to lose his lands to a brother who turned Protestant.

Though this was a history without documents, it constituted in my father's mind a faithful and important record of real things. And it was from this that inevitably I drew a sense of myself in the world, and I never questioned any of it.

Chapter Three

Last night I lent my Indian motorbike to Tom Quaye again, because he was going off to a dance in Osu. He lives in a little tin house at the back of the palm trees somewhere, just a minute away. He was wearing a suit so sharp it would have stunned the natives west of the Shannon.

He just loves that motorbike, as I do myself.

'Now, major, if you don't want me riding that motorbike,' he said, 'you just say. Just because I am seating myself on it does not mean I think it is mine.'

I knew exactly what he meant.

I have told him a few times that I don't exactly have the right to the title major, now the war is over, but he doesn't pay any heed to that.

He displays a very agreeable solicitousness towards me. I wonder what it is about me that causes that. I always think I am hiding my feelings with perfect success, but apparently, no, my heart beats plainly on my sleeve. Otherwise I can't account for Tom Quaye's kindness, which I think is real – I mean, not the 'kindness' of an employee.

'I am going to bring you soon to hear that Highlife music,' he said this morning. 'Highlife music is good for a man. You can drive and I will go on the back,' he said, as if he wasn't absolutely sure this would be the case.

Then to dispel this whole matter for the moment, he sang quietly, quickly, and very tunefully:

Ghana, we now have freedom,
Ghana, land of freedom,
Toils of the brave and the sweat of their labours,
Toils of the brave which have brought results.

Then he raised an imaginary saxophone to his head, and if it wasn't the very spit of my brother Tom, years ago in his dancehall at Strandhill, I don't know what would be. I was laughing then, from the sheer memory of that, superimposed on this present moment.

'You better watch out, Tom, or I'll be singing "Faith of Our Fathers". Then you'll be sorry,' I said.

'I think a man should sing. What we are here for on this earth if not for singing? Singing and dancing. Otherwise everything is so-so *yeye*,' he said, breaking into pidgin. 'I tell you, ever since my wife she left me, if I was not singing I would go crazy.'

Krezy, he pronounced it, *krezy*. Pure Roscommon. Pure Ghana.

The truth is I shouldn't be here in Ghana. I should be at home in Sligo, sorting out something for my children. I should be there, even on the margins, ready to help, ready to advise. That is what a father can do. Instead I am lurking here in Africa like a broken-down missionary, without church or purpose, and merely holding off the hour of my leaving. No wonder Mr Oko, with his kind face, looked at me so strangely when I told him I intended to stay on a while. Why would I? My work here is over.

My heart though, my heart is broken. I know it is. For nearly four years I have laboured through life with this broken heart, but it just gets worse and worse, like an engine with a neglected fault that weakens all the other parts. Now I must try and mend it, I must. I must go back over everything and find the places where it broke and ask the god of good things to mend me, if that is possible. Write it down honestly in this old minute-book of the now defunct Gold Coast Engineering and Bridge-Building Company. Then the man who goes back to Ireland will be a better man, a mended man. That is my prayer now.

An hour ago I rose from the table and went out onto the veranda. A little wind was skipping through the leaden humours of the yard, the wind that, if I remember rightly, means the approach of the rains.

'(What Did I Do to Be So) Black and Blue' . . . Talk about honesty. That was Louis Armstrong here in Accra of all places, last year, as the pot of freedom was boiling. Dropped in from the heavens like a black god. A big open-air concert in Osu. Satchmo smiling, smiling. How Tom would love to have been there, my brother Tom I mean. Tom Quaye probably was, I must ask him. The white wives laughed with delight at the sheer musicality of it all, a few inches from the black wives, laughing with the same delight.

I drove home to Sligo in the Austin – I remember the dusty, baked-cake smell of the leather seats, as I took regretted 'short cuts' across high bog roads – the weekend after my first conversation with Mai, and told my mother about her. And said how hopeless it was, how impossible.

'Why don't you bring her to the magic-lantern show, you *amadán*,' my mother said. She was in the parlour, pasting little cuttings and items that had caught her interest into a scrapbook. It was dark in the little room, but that curious darkness where you can somehow see everything, as if we were turned briefly into cats. That is the dark I think of when I think of my mother. She is probably sitting there now as I write this.

'What?' I said.

'The magic-lantern show, Jack.'

'Mam, Mam, there's no magic-lantern show now, it's "the pictures".'

My mother was not old, but she affected oldness. She had wonderful red hair. She had had me when she was only seventeen. Tom had a job at the picture house in Sligo, so she knew well what I meant. Maybe she preferred the old things.

'Merciful hour, what do I know about modern times? But I tell you, Jack, when she gets a hoult of an understanding of you, everything will be hunky-dory.'

'There's no chance on earth she will go to the pictures with the likes of me,' I said.

So I lay in wait for her again, like a veritable Dick Turpin.

She didn't even speak when she saw me, just gave a sort of *heh* sound, as if to say, I thought you'd be here. Hoped, even? There was a bright, cheery look to her anyhow, she seemed happy enough to see me. My heart tumbled down into my polished black boots, then soared straight back up to the trilby hat on my head. I had no interest in that moment in geology or engineering – just a week before the two passions of my existence. It was all the science of Mai for me then.

Her shoulders in the dark blue dress made me tremble – invisibly, I hoped and prayed. It was the strange sense of hard bone and possibly yielding grace. Her bosom swelled in the embroidered placket of the bodice. It dizzied me. Her black eyes, her hair as black as worry. Her skin which I believe could be called olive-coloured, but so soft it made me wild to touch it, to smooth her cheek with a desolate hand, though I kept my hands fiercely at my sides. Olives of old Mediterranean hillsides, glimpsed from the deck of my ship when I was away with the merchant navy as a youngster, before ever I thought of going to the university . . .

'Well?' she said, with her touch of gentleness that I was beginning to recognise, a condiment, a medicine of gentleness – mixed with the fierceness.

'I was wondering now if you would like to come with me to the Gaiety, to see the show on Saturday? Rin Tin Tin.'

I didn't even think I was speaking English any more. I was surprised when she seemed to understand me.

'Rin Tin Tin,' she said, as a person might recite a sacred creed. 'I like Rin Tin Tin. I am not so sure about you, in your funny old car-coat, and your driving gloves sticking out of your pocket.'

Oh, she was observant. Indeed I had perched my

gloves on the rim of my pocket, so that she might see I had such accoutrements. I blanched with embarrassment.

'I'm not going to be hard on you, Jack McNulty,' she said, perhaps regretting causing such blatant distress. 'Sometimes I talk with too much force. I'm only teasing really.' Then a little pause. 'I like you.'

'If you would do me the honour,' I said, 'I would be a happy man.'

'I don't know anything about that,' she said.

'How do you mean?' I said.

'Making other people happy is a mug's game,' she said. Maybe, now I think of it, I should have listened to her, parsed then and there what she was saying, but there was that wild wave like something advancing on an extremity of Ireland, the Maharees say, pouring through me, jolting every atom in my blood. Her habitual abruptness I could see now was a form of honesty, a species of communication that a person might be well advised to attend to carefully, a Morse signal that needed urgent interpretation. How often as a mere boy in the bowels of ships I had attended to Morse messages in the radio operator's room, ever alert for a Mayday signal. But I wasn't heeding any of that now. It was the undertow of kindness in her voice that was drawing me to her, drowning me, delightfully.

'I have to get home,' she said. 'I like to be there when my father comes back from work.'

'I could run you home in the Austin,' I said, on an inspiration, with a feigned nonchalance.

'No,' she said, just that, the bare word.

'It would be no bother,' I said.

'No,' she said, 'I like to walk in the wind, so I do.'

Then I was more or less obliged to stand aside and let her pass. I had offered her everything I could think of, almost everything I possessed, up to that point. I wanted to pass a chain around her leg and the other end about my own leg. I wanted us to be bound together, in such a fashion that there would be escape for neither of us. It was a strange, wild desire. Even as I tried not to stare at her, I was staring, staring.

She was six feet past me when I drew up a last sentence from the well of myself.

'I'll ask you again next week, if you don't mind. Just in case.'

'Just in case what?' she said, stopping in exasperation, or with an emotion that I assumed was exasperation. She was suddenly vehement, forceful, turned to me again, her feet planted on the cobbles. She might have been about to draw a six-gun on me.

'Just in case what?' she repeated, rather crazily I thought. The lovely black eyes searing me.

'You change your mind,' I said.

'Do you think I'd ever change my mind?' she said. 'Do I look like the shilly-shallying sort?' she said, without the odd anger now, just plain as day, even somewhat surprised.

'You certainly do not.'

I had spoken so forcefully it gave me a fright. Without meaning to, I laughed. Maybe without meaning to also, she laughed as well. A heap of stray wind from the river broke against us both in that moment, her right hand reached up to pull her coat closed, one of my hands dashed to secure my hat. She shook her head then, still laughing, and turned about, walked on, still laughing, her head thrown a little back, much to my delight, much to my delight, laughing, laughing.

The next time I asked her to go out with me it seemed I had fulfilled the list of the necessary efforts a young man must make, and she agreed.

Rin Tin Tin had gone the way of all last week's films, and there was a ferocious weepie on instead. In the foyer, for reasons that are now lost, I fetched out a photograph of myself that I had brought to show her. It was of me, about sixteen, in my white uniform, standing with the other officers on board ship somewhere in the Straits Settlements.

'Well,' she said, without detectable irony, 'you look lovely. You really do.' She had quite lit up at the sight of me, and I was immensely pleased. 'What did you have to do in that uniform?'

'I was a radio operator. It was a two-year course, but I got through it in six weeks.'

She mercifully allowed this boast to go by unmocked.

'You look about twelve,' she said.

'I was only sixteen.'

'The uniform is very youthening,' she said, linking my arm to go into the cinema.

'Yes,' I said.

'Such a lovely young fellow,' she said, laughing, quite mysterious, but very, very delightful.

Chapter Four

When I started to bring her almost weekly to the cinema in Galway I realised the pictures were something of a religion for her. There were a dozen photographs of the stars on the walls of the foyer, and she knew all the names, like a good Russian would know the icons in her local church. Something poured down on her from those staring eyes, and she indeed had something of the same, looking up at them.

'The Town Hall' they called it. It looked like an old palace in the Orient, and smelled of face-powder, disinfectant, and dead mice. The front-of-house usher would have given Tom Quaye a run for his money in the sergeant-major stakes.

Now we were talking like lunatics, in the first voluble flood of love. She was interested in everything, in a way perhaps that I was not. I lived in a sort of lowered ignorance about politics, and truth to tell, politics, even during the civil war, seemed to happen on the fringes of everything, in the corner of your eye if anywhere. History was the burnt edges of the Book of Life, as if it had indeed been in a great fire, but it was not the story itself.

And the troubles my brother Eneas had endured as regards politics had caused a sort of silence in me around such questions, up till now. But Mai was passionately interested in and supported the new government, and was constitutionally able to do nothing except worship at the altar of Michael Collins, who it turned out was a kind of family friend, through an aunt in Cavan. Luckily my brother Tom was an enthusiastic Collins man, too, so I was able to offer his opinions as my own, as it were, in what I hoped was an allowable subterfuge.

'This old country needs a new lick of paint,' she would say, with fervour, her face glowing, as if still staring at the pictures of the stars, and Collins I am sure was mingled in her imagination with Gary Cooper and the like.

'When I get my degree,' she would say, 'I am going to try and get a post in government, you see if I don't. I may teach for a few years and then somehow make my presence felt in Dublin, and then . . .'

The 'and then' was a little vague, but her ambitions were honest and inspiring.

One night, maybe six weeks into our courtship – if that was what it was, we never put a name on it – she told me she was bringing me home afterwards to meet her father. To be informed of this without notice gave me a dreadful fright. She herself was dressed as if for a royal occasion, but she always was anyway, she would have given Lillian Gish a run for her money. Luckily I had recently bought a fine coat with a leather collar, and my best trilby, grey as an otter, was set at an angle on my head. She had a garnet bracelet on one wrist like drops of blood, and a short string of pearls around her neck, jewellery her father had bought her.

Her father.

A young man who has been a radio operator, with two years' service, will have a bit of money saved up. Despite the great expense now of going to the university, I still had a few pounds in the bank. I hoped her father would recognise the splendour of this.

I didn't pay complete heed to the picture on the screen. I sat beside her and watched, in the strange privacy that a cinema bestows on a person, her face held up to the lights and shadows. The white powder she had rubbed on it gave it the sheen and silver of the flower honesty. She had a subtle net on her black hair, with tiny bits of tinsel on it that took the light briefly as her head stirred. She smiled, she frowned, she cried, but all in some otherworldly state, as if she were asleep with her eyes open, or I were asleep and dreaming her.

After the picture we stepped out on vulnerable leather soles into a street that was flooded by a savage temper tantrum of summer rain, a great, moving varnish of glistening black.

'Let's go into Rabbitt's a minute and wait for this to

stop,' I said, not usually inclined to bring her to a public house – not something I thought Mr Kirwan would approve of for his daughter.

I was grateful for the excuse of the rain because I was in need of courage from any source I could find. I put her into the snug with a few other rain-bedraggled women, furnished her with a red lemonade, and went on into the bar proper with its line of dark men, and asked for two whiskies, which I drank down smartly.

Then I felt ready, or at least more ready.

※

I haven't been able to write anything for the last three days. I haven't been able to do much except breathe in and out.

One afternoon about three years ago, I suddenly decided to give up drinking entirely. It just came to me, as I walked as usual towards the clubhouse, that it was time. I turned on my heel and went back home. After nearly forty years of drinking. The strange thing was, I barely missed it, I felt no pain in giving up, it just seemed the right thing to do, and I was able to do it.

Tom Quaye knows as well or better than I do that the rains are imminent and that once they start to hammer down there won't be much point setting off on the Indian, because this end of town will turn into a quagmire. There is a semblance of paving here and there, but it will be all drenched clothes and ruined boots, and even Tom couldn't steer the Indian through the mud and leaps of the sudden rivers that will shortly rule over everything and everyone.

So I didn't have too much of a defence against his suggestion to go with him into Osu in search of a relaxing evening. In fact he filled me so full of dread about the coming rain that for the first time I felt uneasy about being here alone, though I have managed pretty well these many months. So I rashly set out with him, an hour after sundown, with a fulsome, heavy red light still sitting in the sky, and the very green of the plants queerly blazing, myself having given way to Tom's hunger for the handlebars, and perched myself on the flimsy pillion.

And off we went, looking more like a comedy duo than either of us would wish, some curious Stan and Ollie, though hopefully this was just in my mind. I had to hold onto his old khaki shirt, and had the opportunity to notice the remarkable number of holes in the back of it, as if rats had got at a grain sack.

We stopped by his little quarters and in the shortest imaginable time he was out again in that sharp suit I had seen before, his hair slicked down till it was as shiny now as a beetle under his hat and, when we arranged ourselves again on the motorbike, smelling of some pungent, potent oil.

A sort of grimness had descended on Tom as if he were burdened now with the responsibility to entertain me, and I did my best with scraps of sentences and little broken comments offered from the pillion to relieve him of it. Maybe he was reconsidering bringing this balding, ageing Irish ex-major into the night world of Osu, but if he was, he didn't say. And when we reached the better stretch of road between our district and Osu, he opened up the throttle on the motorbike, and seemed to find a better, gayer gear in himself too. Under his breath he was singing as he usually did some little song to himself, this time in his own tongue of Ewe.

Soon we were weaving and cutting through a great host of Saturday-night souls making a tremendous ruckus in the streets of Osu. We swept past the Regal cinema, which I was noticing for the first time – Mai would have clocked it long since. The sullen, sunken presence of the Atlantic shore, a vast silken darkness over to our left, framed this oddly neat back end of a place, with its tin houses and improvised lights, its Tilley lamps and generators, and suddenly my mind was filled with memories of Sligo nights, the traps with their big lamps taking the short cut to Strandhill across the wide expanse of tidal sand, if the moon was accommodating, my friends and acquaintance calling out to each other, driven almost mad by anticipation of the dancing. And the Fords and Austins taking to the sand like dimly shining animals, blinding the cold bands of walkers, trudging on, trudging on, after the long, long walk from the town, holding onto their wind-ravaged hats in the banging storm and the sleeting rain, the lovelier girls flagging down lifts that would rescue them from such torrents and sorrows. And Mai as alive as any living person ever was, radiating simple human joy.

Tom steered us to a safe spot to leave the Indian, courteously gave me the keys, and we bumped and apologised our way into a premises glorying in the name of The Silver Slipper. I was mollified in my creeping worry about what I was doing there at all by the fact that 'The Silver Slipper', in the guise of *'An Slipear Airgid'*, was my father's favourite jig tune on the flute, not to mention the name of a famous dancehall in Bundoran.

Once in the door, and two tickets bought for pennies, the crowd oozed through a corridor and then, as if carried on floodwater, spread out into a big room with instantly confusing lights, and a band playing Tom's Highlife music on a wide stage. What at first seemed a roaring whirlpool of dancers, when you got eyes for it resolved into men in loose white suits like Tom's, and women in their bright summer dresses, the whole a sort of conspiracy to bamboozle and knock you senseless as you came in.

Tom's friends were there, in jubilant spirits. A friendly lot, though God knows what they really made of me.

There was an extremely pretty woman among them, who leaned forward to greet me with a gentleness that shocked me. I realised I had been living the life of a virtual prisoner. But all I seemed to feel was panic. I accepted the first tin of palm wine offered to me, and drained it.

Then the evening slipped into a new gear, so familiar to me from countless nights throughout my drinking days. My drinking days, had there been any other kind of days? In the last few years, yes, is my own answer to myself.

New swirls and deluges of colour were added to the real motions and joys of the room. One hour roared after another. At some point my head must have stopped recording anything. I have a blurred memory of bits of dark road and things looming up, and that smell of Tom's hair oil mixed up in the memory, like it was some crazy salad of odds and ends, of glimpses and shards. And then nothing, nothing, nothing, and a sudden, vague sense of horror at snatched-at recollections, who was that I had been holding and kissing in the whirling darkness, or did I dream that, why for a while did I have the sense that someone was sitting on me, what in the name of hell was that? And then nothing, nothing again, and nothing.

And then in the bright glare of morning, opening my eyes to find myself in my bed, with the mosquito curtains all in disarray, and my stomach bare to the world, and my pyjamas strewn, I could just see, on the writing table in the next room, and a long, horrifying piss mark on the polished floor, and all along my arms, my belly, and my feet, the red marks of mosquitoes. And in the centre of the floor, queerly self-possessed, the pyramid of a turd.

And then probably what woke me, the sound of Tom Quaye coming in to work, and me making a wild lunge towards the blessed turd, for pity's sake, for pity's sake to cover it, so my shame would not be made manifest, and yet Tom getting in the door innocently before I could reach it, and opening his arms, the spectacle before him of his naked employer, in mid-leap, and him saying, in kindness and astonishment, searing me to the marrow:

'Major, you shit on the floor?'

I am staring out the window at the searing yard outside. A large fly, as black as a railing, a moment ago staggered and stopped in mid-air, such is the mighty hand of the heat. The weather is a sort of celestial pointsman.

My head is empty. It is a little moment before thought, I suppose. Before thoughts rush in again. A thousand times I have felt this in my life. It has little to do with true peace, it's the body recovering from the onslaught of alcohol.

When you are alone, there is a special quality to this, I find. I was drunk alone, I felt guilt alone, and now I feel this deceitful peace alone, for which nevertheless I am grateful.

Here is my little library, ranged along my work table, complete with two huge dead moths, and a brick-sized beetle that didn't have the strength fully to retrieve his wings before he died:

Bridges and Structural Design.
Bengal Lancer, by F. Yeats-Brown.
Barrack-Room Ballads.
Foundations of Bridges and Buildings, by Jacoby and Davis.
Hound of Heaven.

Chapter Five

'The *buveur* of Sligo' Mai's father used to call me, though not in my hearing. Today the phrase came winging back to me.

Those heavy rooms of Grattan House, weighted down by the accumulated bullion of her father's life, the sideboard in the dining room for instance, I could see the floorboards cupping under its crouching legs and lion's paws, and Mrs Kirwan had given each bare foot of everything, chair and table and whatnot, a little embroidered covering. The whole room looked like it might break into movement nonetheless, the sideboard walk forward, the chair make for the door, but they didn't, everything held its breath, it felt like, and the vast cornucopia of silken scarves that was the bay outside stirred and heaved in the wide windows, shrouded all the same in sun-faded and dusty-looking curtains. Those heavy rooms, and myself entering them for the first time, with Mai just ahead, and the quick little change in her somehow that I detected, almost with an unwanted sixth sense, a distance made between her and me, as if disowning me temporarily in the aura, the principality of her father. Her block heels banging across the dark boards. Her mother, bony as a cat, with her child's smile, as if no one was looking at her, as if she was in some measure invisible, in a dress so old-fashioned it seemed a mistake had been made in time, and we were walking into the 1880s. My own good shoes with their heel-plates and metal studs to give them wear, beating out a smaller tattoo than Mai's across the floor, yet too much noise to make me comfortable or easy. And then the room itself, the smell of fried plaice and cabbage, as it turned out, and the two waiting, the diminutive mother, and the utterly present father, with his waist-coat and his stomach, and his Dundrearies, his chin shaved clean, and his head bald, and the sudden riot of horse-black hair along his cheeks, and his face turned in a certain way, expectant, but maybe also ready to strike, the *paterfamilias*, the solid man, with his air of tremendousness, and his agreeable Galway voice of a man who bought things in shops and hadn't to worry too much about the price, and you could sense *his* father a shadow at his side, a similar substantial man, and his father too, a double shadow, and all the way back to when Macs and O's like myself were banned from the streets of the city, but I could see it in the eyes too, large, trout-dark, the quiet welcome and the stern dismissal, like a failed harmony in a song.

For all that Mai was bringing me into her house – her

father's favourite child – for all that my coat had leather on the collar, the gold tie-pin a diamond on it, for all that I had travelled the seas of the earth, drank my beer in Galveston and the ports of the Straits Settlements, I prayed he wouldn't think me a ragamuffin, a potential assassin of the life of his daughter. By force of character I hoped to carry the day, but I knew it would be tricky for me to prosper in that house.

Which was why I had stopped the Austin again at the old hotel in Salthill and downed another double. Which was why I was fairly indifferent to the event by the time I suffered it, and took the questioning of her father more or less under the anaesthetic of four whiskies.

Mr Kirwan spoke about his work, about the people of Galway, and indeed about the people of Sligo, where he also did business. About the great reluctance of a certain class of Sligo person to buy insurance.

'There are people, you see, who do not think much about the future. They cannot be made to live sensibly even in the present.'

Then her mother spoke very pleasantly about Collins and I could see that Mai's politics had not sprung out of nowhere. Her mother seemed nervous, yes, but extremely loving towards Mai, and even as she spoke she moved unasked various dishes and items towards her daughter. Now Mai also began to speak, talking of things that I didn't wholly understand, mentioning people familiar to her and her parents, places, times, events. She spoke though as a grown-up, not a child, as if she was expected to hold views, and as strong as she liked. Her father was not afraid to vex her with contrary opinions, and now launched into a long speech about the horrors of the civil war, which just lately had affected Salthill itself, with some poor hotelier dragged out and shot, by which side and for what reason I could not make out.

John Redmond, the leader of the old Irish Party at Westminster, had been the man, I surmised, for Mr Kirwan, but he was dead, and all that old dream was gone. Mr Kirwan wasn't comfortable with countries won by force of arms.

'But sure, Dad,' said Mai, 'Michael Collins is just John Redmond with guns.'

'Yes,' he said, 'yes,' vehemently in that forgotten Galway night, 'and isn't that the problem, isn't that the whole problem, Mai?'

'But, Dad, didn't John Redmond form the Volunteers, and didn't he arm them against the Ulstermen?'

'Well, well, he never intended to use them,' said her father.

'I think if you have guns you should use them,' said Mai triumphantly, 'if only to keep them from becoming unsafe.'

'You can keep them perfectly safe by oiling them,' said her father sagely.

And on and on, pleasantly, buoyantly.

I didn't say so aloud, but I knew my own father didn't really care what bugger was in government, although he had liked the old king, and was sad that he was gone. 'People don't seem to notice the efforts the king made to have peace in Ireland,' he used to say, his fiddle or his piccolo poised between tunes.

Suddenly though I felt emboldened to speak, because a plan was forming in my mind, which was maybe to go out to Africa with Mai when we were married – well, if we were ever married, I had to say to myself, sitting there in that company.

'I am just grateful that we are still bound somewhat to the crown.'

'What do you mean, Jack?' Mai said, laughing.

'By the oath of allegiance and so on. The king is still the head of state. I think that is a good thing, all in all.'

Although Mr Kirwan did not exactly baulk at this, he seemed troubled by it. He seemed to need to make a great effort to tease this thought of mine out. But it was difficult for him, because he obviously did not wish to offend, but at the same time could not agree with me.

I was having my own difficulties. I sat in an armless chair while he pursued his ideas, an armless chair with a nearly legless man. The whisky, having made a subtle and deceptive entry into my bloodstream, had now stirred those little rivers up, and whatever organs it reached and touched in the body, it revved them up mercilessly, so that my heart pounded, my temples I was quite sure were visibly throbbing, and some kind of rather pleasant rictus claimed my upper legs, so that they wanted, independently of myself, to kick vigorously the underside of the table. This I managed to control. But the long, wide expanse of the table swam in its deep polish, like a pool under dark trees, and when I lifted my sweating hands from the wood, I saw I had left twelve little whorled impressions on it.

Mr Kirwan had taken the longer route through his speech, and somewhere in the seventh or eighth minute of it he had circled back to his views on insurance and the recalcitrant people of Sligo, with his wife smiling her nervy smile, and Mai frowning now neutrally and carefully eating her plaice.

'And I am sure it is because of all this that many a Sligo family, many a bereaved wife, with her brood of children, has suffered the consequence of the reluctance of your common or gardener Sligoman to make proper provision for his family.'

I could somehow imagine him giving this speech long ago, on the Magheraboy Road, say, on a rainy February evening in Sligo, or out in Strandhill village with its cliff-edge economies, and never forgetting his lack of success with it, among the ungrateful citizens. But I wasn't paying absolute attention to him, I was looking at Mai as she ate with minute fierceness, marvelling at her, wondering what her true purpose was now, her true condition, was she suffering, was she keeping her head down, was it all passing off with great effect, I couldn't tell. And then my mind was wandering out through the windows and mentally down the long sloping garden to the sea-wall, and I sensed the callows beyond the wall, and was thinking of those notorious high tides of spring and autumn, and could just see the water breast the wall, and pour over onto the rose bushes and the violets, all in my mind's eye, not a real flood at all, and I was smiling then, with a whisky smile, all was right with the world, and I suddenly said, not entirely disconnected from what Mr Kirwan was saying, but somewhat, I suppose:

'I sincerely doubt it.'

Just that, not spoken with perfect diction, slurred no doubt, and maybe it was the blatant slurring that offended him, but he stopped speaking, or rather, declined to speak further, he sat there in his carving chair, with its two splendid arms, and under the plain antimacassar, which my mother would love to have adorned, a blank coat of arms, as if waiting for the final carving, the final ennoblement of the Kirwans, or despairing of it, despairing of the hidden and secret middle classes of Ireland. And he looked at me with an open, smileless look, that didn't need words, that had all the appearance of a final judgement, on this bloody Jack McNulty, the *buveur* of Sligo, that he be cast forever into the deepest and dampest dungeon, and the keys thrown away.

For if Mai was to be given every latitude in her ideas and her remarks, I suddenly realised, too late, that her dubious beau certainly was not.

After dinner, in the ashes of everything, Mai played a Schubert nocturne ('Not the famous one,' she said) on an ancient, perfectly maintained upright piano. It was the same dark, dark brown as a dress which, for some reason she didn't offer, she had changed into. The music was slow and melancholy, a nocturne played in the very last night-time of her childhood, no, surely well into the dawn of proper womanhood, and I saw her father crying in his chair, and her mother wept, and so did I, while Mai played on, with a dry eye.

Not a great success, all told. But the strange thing was, there was nothing about Frank Kirwan that I didn't like. I might have been the specimen ultimately stuck by his pin, but he was a deeply agreeable man, I could see, in essence. I would love to have met with his approval. I would love to have sat with him early and often.

Although I am not sure her father ever changed his

opinion of me much, he was stalwart enough of soul to endure me at first, and thenceforth I was often in their house, even if it was only to talk to her mother in the parlour with the ease of the admired person – for indeed her mother was always very kind to me – while Mr Kirwan occupied somewhere in the house what was referred to as his study.

I was in a position of knowledge now to note certain things about the Kirwans. It wasn't all quite as it seemed, but nearly. He sold shilling insurances to all and sundry but being a Kirwan could count himself among the famous Tribes of Galway. Mai loved his aloofness and his lack of the common touch. Perhaps not so handy in an insurance man, and Mai's mother took in paying lodgers in the summer months, though there was no sign to say so outside the house. It was very discreet. The rains and winds of summer lashed across Salthill with the air of an accepted catastrophe, but it was officially a seaside resort. And indeed there were always a few days that burned with hope and sun, and all in all it was a different world from my father's, in his little cramped house on John Street, his job at the Lunatic Asylum, his dancing band, and his indirect wife.

One of the things that put me deeper in love with Mai was her own love for her father. I wondered if I could earn such a depth of love, win it from her as it were, as time passed. While Mai often puzzled me, because she was after all a myriad and complicated person, I admired her tremendously, more and more indeed as the months went on. Her gifts were substantial, her mind was neither deceitful nor shallow, and as for depths, they certainly in her were never hidden. I thought she was the most considerable individual I had ever encountered. She had times of gentleness so complete and profound, she not only took my breath away, she took my heart, my soul, my very purpose in being alive. She took it all to herself and I was proud that she had done so.

I come back to this an hour later. I am shaken to remember myself, gauche and not very sober in that vanished room. Those two people, Mr and Mrs Kirwan, long dead, and yet the memory of that awkward dinner still with the power to dismay me. To be rejected, for a moment of firmness ill-advised, misplaced. But should a Sligoman not defend his fellow Sligomen? What was it about a mere small phrase like that that offended him so? Was there something else, that I missed? Something out of place? Flies open, I dread to think. My accent not right, my eyes, my soul, my youth? Did he suddenly sense something about me in a curious floating text above my head? What I might do to his beloved daughter, the effect a man's drinking might have on her – West of Ireland drinking, diligent, unrestrained, the antidote to the dark rains and the year-long winter? If so, I can find some sympathy for him, as a father myself. And for her gentle, light-hearted mother, who nevertheless seemed to suffer sometimes in her mind – withdraw to her own room for days on end, sitting on the edge of a narrow single bed, looking out on the great wordless theatre of Galway Bay, unless the words were the secret words of God.

A memory I have carried with me like the little creature that gets into the apple barrel, climbs in all unseen, and by the time your ship reaches Madagascar and the provisioner opens the barrel, there is not one apple left integral and whole.

Chapter Six

When my brother Tom was still a teenager he got a job as the organist at the Picture House in Sligo. It is not given to every man to see his brother in such a guise. The owners had gone full out for their effects, including the installation of hydraulic lifts very interesting to me as a young engineering student. These had been invented during the First World War as a way to raise a Zeppelin undercarriage – so my text book said.

Three hundred faces raised and expectant, the motley population of Sligo that could afford the sixpence for a ticket. It began in Stygian darkness, then a mighty release of sound somewhere under the earth, then the floor of the fore-stage opened, and a geyser of light burst upward, like a veritable explosion. Then an engine was seen rising, bearing the great organ, then my brother, if it was my brother now really, in his blazing white suit, his army-like cap, his stocky frame, his still back and his arms distorted by light into the wide thick arms of a gorilla, powerful as Zeus, working the keys like a wizard, and he seemed to be sitting astride the sun itself, such a great flower of light forced its way out, blazing and frantic, wonderfully lunatic, then noise upon noise, and more noise, then, with a calculated majesty, he let it all go, stopped it all, so that for a moment the breath was burned out of the audience, like the force of a detonation, their hearts paused, their hopes were held suspended, the past had no sting, just for a moment, just for a moment, and then life was given back, the first scenes of the film flashed and flared into life, and Tom would throw the kindling of one note into the silence, the little Lucifer of a note, graciously allowing us reprieve, our knees settling down again, here and there a redeemed soul clearing their throat, a little laughter here and there, a brave man somewhere giving his date a quick squeeze, her cry of surprise, and then laughing, the great bliss of it, the life and death of it, the death and life, and my brother Tom the captain of it.

The Plaza, Strandhill. My father Old Tom, my brother Young Tom, their dancehall. Sometimes I imagine that everyone's to be found there still, everyone that was important to me, Tom and Eneas, the girls we thought we were in love with, the girls we definitely were in love with, lovely Roseanne, vivid and vibrant Mai, and what was the name of the girl Eneas loved, wasn't it Viv, it was, eternally present in those tin walls, the to-do and turmoil of the Atlantic oftentimes lending the little orchestra inside an added music, the ferocious tantrums and deceitful moods and sudden violence and queer hatreds and manias of the sea. But of course it is all long ago, and a hundred different fates and stories have swallowed up my comrades, as my own fate has swallowed me. We are in the great belly of the whale of what happens, we mistook the darkness for a pleasant night-time, and the phosphorescent plankton swimming there for stars.

Mai dancing there, in her youth. What immense pride I felt in her, so happy to show her off to my friends and my brother. Even as he struck out the notes from his trumpet, I could see his eyes following her. She loved all the new American dances and could do them to the nth degree into the bargain, and I was well-nigh obliged to learn them quick. Such joy in that, her strength, her fiery steps, her willingness to allow for my lack of polish, as long as I would thunder through the hours with her, mashing our arms and legs, with that measured wildness. Her face aglow, her stamina infinite, always eager to take up the gauntlet of the next dance. Her face glistening in the helpful darkness, her eyes all ember and turf-black, her body swirling in her smart dresses, turning and leaping, her legs as strong as a circus performer, lovely firm legs, her delicate hands, her habit of happiness, her radiant and infective joy.

Mai made friends with everyone, as if her life depended on it. I was warmly congratulated, in her hearing and out of her hearing both, as if I had done a great thing in finding her. But I knew my luck too. I felt like the luckiest man in Sligo, in Ireland.

Roseanne, who was actually the piano player in Tom's band, and of course his sweetheart, Mai especially liked, not only because they knew a lot of the same music, but because Roseanne herself was as pretty as a film star, and shone with youth and beauty, different from Mai's, but as mysterious. Unusually enough, she was a Presbyterian. When she was younger she had been a waitress in the Café Cairo and I suppose every young man in Sligo had been soft on her, including myself.

It was the great fortune of our youth that such girls were there in Sligo, living and breathing, and willing to give us the time of day, and, when it came to dancing anyhow, the time of night.

And Tom at that time was just getting going at the politics, and was hoping to get elected to the town council when the civil war calmed down, if it ever did, and Mai was fascinated by all that, a person in front of her who she thought really would be able to get things done, to give the country the lick of paint she yearned for. When all would be made new, spruced up, and the future shine before us like the path the moon made on the sea at the Rosses.

Then streaming out to the cars and taking our way

back to Sligo town along the white roads of Strandhill, gleaming in the moonlight, skirting the brimming tide of the estuary, and then myself content to surge through the small hours across bog and small farms to Galway city, to get her safely home to her father's house. Mai tired as a child after a long day, and sober as a child, never touching a drop of drink, never, her body warm against me in the car, as the windscreen wiper lashed away the rain, and I hunched forward, peering into the shattered darkness.

The ingredients of nothing maybe, nothing at all – but everything, everything that at close of day we value, everything.

Do I imagine it all? Was there really such happiness? There was, there was.

Towards the end of the year Michael Collins was killed in Cork. The bullet might as well have passed through his body and into all the countless hearts that loved him, like Mai's. She had loved him, the idea of him, and the future that he seemed to hold in his gift, as Mai saw it. But they killed him.

✿

Suspecting that Tom Quaye would be a better historian than myself of my lapse from grace, I have been trying to draw him out about our night in Osu, but he is a very difficult man to get to talk when he has no desire to. He listens, staring me straight in the eye, but then he just turns his head and goes about some other business.

Today he put a new element in one of the Tilley lamps, then for some reason, though I tried to dissuade him, he hauled out my old cavalry boots from the cupboard, one of the few remaining things of my army uniform, which I brought out with me this time thinking they would be handy as mosquito boots. But even in the dozen years since the war ended, I find my calves have increased in girth to such a degree that I cannot accommodate the boots on them. I can get them on but cannot get myself out of them again, as if my legs were corks in wine bottles and nary a corkscrew handy. Then Tom Quaye is pulling at them, with me being dragged slowly across the floor, chair and all, till, poof! the leg gives up and surrenders the wretched boot. So they live a dark and dusty life in the cupboard now. But Tom Quaye has a thing about polishing them, and this afternoon he carried them forth into the light and rather angrily I thought lashed on the polish, and then worked away mightily with a cloth to give them a barrack-room shine. But all wasted work really.

And all the while this was going on, it was myself trying to draw him out about Osu. There were little snatches and sparking illuminations and ill-remembered moments of it that were still bothering me. I tried first to winkle a way in by talking about his beloved Highlife music, which only launched him into a panegyric about E. T. Mensah, the man who wrote 'Freedom Highlife', part of Tom's 'under his breath' repertoire. Tom, no more than myself, doesn't like to hit nails on the head, seemingly, he likes to come at things sideways, or rather, move away from them sideways. But this is the way of the world. A direct question in the company of men is in most contexts a sort of insult, something you learn young in Sligo bars.

He had got from a woman he called his 'Aunty-aunty' some sort of concoction in a little twist of paper, and, having put the boots back in the cupboard, this he then tipped out on a saucer, mixed it with water, using a tiny salt spoon that I never use for salt, a survivor of a little vanished hoard of such things from my in-laws, and then, really without asking me, undid my white shirt, laid my chest and belly bare, and still talking about Highlife and its byways and main roads, without much in the way of interruption, he proceeded to dab a little button of this stuff on each mosquito bite, which he well knew were causing me tremendous itchiness. My belly in particular was a dreepy constellation of disintegrating red stars. He let this all dry and then he put on my shirt for me again, as if I were suddenly armless myself, and did up the buttons, and, just before he left now for the day, gave what amounted as far as I could see to a bow in my direction, which wordless gesture flummoxed me.

'Thank you, Tom,' I said. 'Jesus, there's great cooling in that stuff, right enough. How much does Aunty-aunty need for it?'

'I will give her sixpence, with your permission, major.'

'You certainly will,' I said, and fetched out the coins from my trousers. 'Oh, there's an old one,' I said, glancing as I always do at the dates of the coins, an old habit. It was a worn, deep-brown penny from 1860, with the head of a youngish Victoria on it. Tom Quaye smiled, but he didn't bother looking at it.

Then he was readying to go off, and not for the first time I felt a little tug of regret. I like having him about. When you live as if you were Robinson Crusoe on his island, everything starts to get gathered into what you have left to you – and what I have at the moment is the friendship of this man, whom of course I pay to come in and do the damn chores. It's not exactly an empire of family and friends. But, remarkably enough, it does me for the moment.

So off he went, singing as is his wont. The door closed on his song, and the mosquito screen rattled against it ineptly like a small child's idea of drumming:

Before it starts raining
The wind will blow
I warned you but you did not listen

Mr Kirwan banned me from the house. There was an unfortunate incident in Sligo town, as he was wending his way home one day from his insurance selling. It was just the worst bit of luck. I suppose he was heading up to the station to retrieve himself from the mean folk of Sligo. It was a bleak, dark evening in December and I had spent the day with pals in Hardigan's Bar. I do remember him vaguely, standing above me in Wine Street, with that same absent stare, and his top hat incongruous against the scudding clouds. I was heeled up like a cart against the wall of the bank building. I couldn't have spoken to him if he had asked me a question, but he didn't bother himself with that. I remember the roar of the Garvoge in the near distance, because it had rained mercilessly for three days and the old river was in flood.

The next morning, before heading up to the university, I discussed the whole matter with my mother.

'Holy Crimea,' she said, for once in no manner optimistic, 'that's not good.'

Then she gave me a sermon about temperance as well she might. Eneas, while still in Ireland before his exile, had been not much of a drinker, but Tom, still a youngster really, and working hard at the cinema and with his father in the band, already drank a deal. Old Tom she laboured to regulate like you might a faulty pump. Whisky was the McNulty drink. I associate it now with those wild blanked-out skies between Strandhill and town, waking up in inclement ditches, then seeking far and wide in the throbbing misery of morning my motorcar, like it was a lost heifer, abandoned somewhere in the muddle and the chaos.

Mr Kirwan pleaded with Mai, he beseeched her, she said, he went down on his knees to her, imploring, imploring. Calling to heaven to help him make her understand the peril she was in. It wasn't the *buveur* of Sligo he called me now, which might have been misinterpreted as vaguely affectionate. He told her that any association with me would be disastrous for her, that I would surely drag her down to the same level in time, and so on, and so on.

But she was telling me this with a strange little laughter running through it. It amused her. We were sitting in the little cafe at the edge of Strandhill beach. I had run her down to Sligo in the Austin and we were going to go to the dance later in the Plaza. The bay there, so primitive and wide, as if desolate and unknown to mankind, with not a house in view, showed us its army upon army of white horses, their white-plumed heads rearing and tumbling on the fierce beaten colours of the water, strange blues and blacks, as if blue and black could be fire, and thrown from these wild acres, the heaven-ascending spray. And myself and Mai sitting at a little table, in a little tin room, our eyes drawn out to the ruckus of the bay as we talked. By deep contrast, the strange calm in her.

'He thinks I am at Queenie Moran's house today,' she said. 'We will just have to be as clever as Aquinas.'

Chapter Seven

Nevertheless when Mai graduated she kept her promise to herself and went to England to teach. She said it would just be for a year. In her Russian coat with the fur collar, her yellow gloves, and the neat cases with her name in gold upon them beside her, her father's gift, she stood in the station looking momentarily woebegone. She stepped in close to me and, lifting a yellow-gloved hand, touched my cheek.

'Take care, Jack,' she said, which sounded both like an endearment and a warning.

'Take care, you, Mai, please.'

And she gave me one of her good kisses.

Then she was alone in the carriage, the frame of the window giving me the sense of an oil painting, a genre picture to assail the heart. Then she blew me a kiss, and nodded her lovely head. The waterfall of her black hair, the hat like a boat trying to weather it, her dark eyes in the dark carriage, not so much absent as deep, deep as a well, with the water a far coin below of brightness and blackness. Looking, looking at me, as the train drew out. Was that a flash of doubt across her features, just for a moment? I was shivering.

What was I going to do without her, what was I going to do without her?

❧

This village of Tom's, called Titikope, somewhere up the Volta river, is both the centre of his world but also the very thing he has lost. I am sure it enjoys its own reality. But it also exists in Tom's inner mind. Though he himself is an element of that imaginative place that has been excluded, he carries it at the heart of himself.

Now I know that his wife's name is Miriam, and that he has a son and daughter. His children are more or less grown, as I calculate it, because they were born before the war.

And it is the war, still, that is Tom's difficulty. Not only in the matter of savings and pensions, but the very effect of going to the war in the first place.

Everything that he says about his war experiences circles back to the fact that he is no longer wanted in his home place by his wife. So that when the dog of his story seems to stray away and meander about, no, it is just an illusion, because in fact it always doubles back to Miriam. He talks about prostitutes and killing, but not because he seems to feel such things are what has caused his dilemma. And they are not, at all. It is something much more mysterious. The largeness of the difference between how he thinks about the world and how I think about it is actually what makes him interesting to me. His guilt is not the usual guilt of a European man like me.

When he first left his village to join the Gold Coast Regiment he had no idea he would be away for three or four years, without any leave. His local chieftain came to the village one evening and, speaking passionately about the English king, and the danger to the Gold Coast from the French in Sierra Leone, moved him to leave his wife and young children and join up, even though he was not particularly young. He told his wife he would be back by the end of the rainy season, or failing that, soon after. Of course he had no idea when he would be back, he knew nothing about that, he knew nothing about the world, he had actually never seen a town before, let alone a place like Accra.

Anyway, before he quite knew what was happening, he and his new comrades were bumped across Africa to Kenya, where they were put in a camp outside Nairobi. Here they sweltered for nine months. Tom took a prostitute to cook for him and share his bed. There was immense rivalry for these women. There were pitched battles on the outskirts of the camp, where men laid into each other with ferocity. White soldiers were involved too, fellas from South Africa and Rhodesia.

Then they were transported through Arabia and India to Burma, where Tom learned to hate the Japanese and give them no quarter. They killed every prisoner they took.

After the war he was a year waiting to be demobbed, stuck in Burma. The war was long over when he got back to the Gold Coast, and his people, hearing no news of him, had presumed he was dead, and had already held their ceremony of mourning. This meant, he said, that he was in fact dead, or at least, a walking ghost. So when he came to the outskirts of his village, and people cast their eyes on him and wailed in wonder and horror, he was sprinkled with sacred dust by the witch doctor, to try to return him to the living.

But Miriam, his wife, had also believed him dead. She didn't think the witch doctor sprinkling him with dust changed anything. In her great fear of the dead she wanted nothing to do with him and asked him to go away again, which, in his grief and confusion, he did.

He returned to Accra and poked about for work. He joined the protest march with his fellow ex-soldiers. He was arrested as an agitator and tortured. It was Mr Oko, as a liaison officer with the UN, that got him out of prison.

Hearing all this, I understood better his relative silence in the first months knowing him. Why would he say any of this to a strange whiteman, when it was better just to get on with the bit of work and keep his history to himself?

✌

Summer brought Mai home. She had written regular and passionate letters to me from the English school. Now she sent me a postcard to meet her at Rosses Point that Sunday. Her great friend Queenie Moran was now working as a district nurse in Sligo, and Mai was able to tell her father she was going down to see her.

I motored out to the Rosses, through a delinquent sequence of sunlight and rain-clouds, and parked on the little headland where the long flight of steps goes down to the strand. The last cars were turning on the sandy clifftop and the walkers heading homeward. The early dark began to take possession of everything. I knew the motor bus didn't come out as far as this, but would be depositing Mai further back along the road, and I got out of the car and waited for her. I was veritably trembling.

But she didn't seem to be coming. I hadn't seen her now for a long time and maybe at Christmas I had had the sense that she wasn't making much of an effort to see me. Maybe the whole thing was over and maybe it was better so. And what was it anyhow, but a mismatch between two people from different worlds? That was a small part of my response, right enough. But the greater part of me was caught now in a tidal surge somewhere between longing and anguish. The salt wind scoured my face, and although the rain held off, you could smell it, and almost see it, walking across the wide acres of the sea below. I felt abandoned. Then suddenly she was there.

'Mai,' I said.

'Jack,' she said. 'It's bloody cold out here. What were we thinking of?'

'I've missed you, Mai, so much,' I said, wondering would I hazard a kiss, or a touch of my hand on her cheek? But she stood there, as if stalled, out of reach somehow, in her fur-collared coat, her hair neatened back and hidden by her hat. She always knew the thing that would suit her. Then she leaned in after all and kissed me, and stood back again. The joy of it, I had to shake my head to get rid of the dizziness she had created. She stood there now, smiling, at her ease. I took the opportunity just to look at her. The face, the eyes I had longed to see again. What is it that starts to bind one soul to another? It is so often like holding an opinion that all the world seeks to refute. But she seemed to me proud, beautiful, and honest. As I stood there in my polished shoes, and my own youth, and regarded her, I knew that I loved her.

We were halfway across the great strand, walking arm in arm, when the deluge struck. She loosened her grip on my arm, and we went careering across the sand, hand in hand, the rain itself as if getting over-excited, leaping at us, and then Mai against my expectation bursting out into laughter, wonderful laughter fulfilling all the adjectives of laughter, pealing, wild laughter, and I knew that it was a genuine delight to her, to be running like that, our leather shoes being ruined by the seawater and the rain, just a kingdom of wetness, till we reached the place she must have been heading for, a cave in the far cliff, which we now threw ourselves into, not a big cave at all, low but enough for me to stand in, with a long sucked-out section where the sea had forced its way in and out, in and out for a million years, beginning long before such creatures as ourselves were on the earth. There, suddenly, she took a hold of me, she just fetched me to her, as if the movement were a peremptory word of some kind, and God knows if we were dressed or naked, I couldn't say, only lunatics would take off their clothes in an Irish summer, the memory itself is the colour of the new darkness and the old rain, we are blanked out there, but she is kissing me, I can lay claim to be the dependable recorder of that, the very historian, and I am kissing her, and the back of my drenched head is lifting, and I am as happy as man ever was, in the whole history of the world, to be present there, to have reached that moment, of being with her, to be the object of her hunger.

Her father was old for a father and in the way of things he died.

There was a big cortège leaving Grattan House, himself in the horse-drawn hearse. They only had to bring him a few yards to the church. Every now and then, as the priest spoke about him, Mai let out a sort of primeval cry. I put my arm around her in the pew and felt the furnace of grief in her.

Her mother was quiet, as if grief had sewn her mouth with a cruel stitch. I was sitting between Mai and her brother Jack, because there was no one to stop me now, and I felt an odd sense of disgrace in being there, though no one among the living said anything untoward.

While her father lived, the only times I was in the house of late were when he was out, and her mother would let me in, either not being of the same mind as her husband on the subject of the *buveur* of Sligo, or not wanting to go against her daughter.

But in the deep winter following, her good mother withered in the empty house, and also died, and the mason chiselled out under her husband's inscription the accustomed words, *And of his wife, Mary.*

After this second funeral, in the parlour, and after

the mourners had gone home, and only her brother Jack remained, sitting in a chair at the top of the landing with his long legs stretched on the window-sill, out of earshot, gazing at the grey expanse of the sea, dark and mildewed, like one of those great mirrors whose silver backing is failing, not much inclined, as was usual for him, to speak, I sat alone with Mai. She was weakened and vulnerable. She looked like a wealthy person from whom everything, lands, houses, money, has been snatched away in a financial cataclysm, sitting there humbly and quietly, her white hands holding her black gloves, her face down, looking at those hands and gloves, as if they might hold the clue to the next thing she should do. I felt oddly like a doctor, and knew instinctively that she was going to trust in my diagnosis. Just for a moment I thought I should show her the mercy of silence, and say nothing. That could have been the loving thing to do. This was a simplified Mai. She was without question the child of those two vanished people, the absolute child, and I do not know if she had the wherewithal in the upshot to be anything else.

'He really was a fine old gentleman,' I said. She raised her face to me when I said it, as if weighing secret things up in a hidden scales. There was a long pause.

'You are gentleman enough, in your own way,' she

said, not quite trying to flatter me, and maybe even believing it in that moment. Then she let her gaze fall again, as if the conversation was over.

'We can be married in the spring,' I said, 'if you wanted.'

She raised her eyes from gazing at her lap and gazed at me as if I were for a strange moment just as inanimate as the gloves.

'I do love you so,' I said.

Her brow creased in a frown and her mouth tightened as though someone had pulled on a little hidden string somewhere in her cheeks. She didn't speak for a full minute. It was one of those times when I was entirely relaxed with her. She was there before me, our knees nearly touching, the black mourning cloth of my trousers nearly joining with the dark, rich brocade of her dress, as if our clothing was marrying first. How can I talk about her now without praising her? Something keeps clearing, clarifying, so that I keep arriving at her without judgement as it were, as now, when I think about her there, and see her in my mind's eye, long ago, when she was young, and her parents had deserted her. And what I see is an essence which is in itself solo and isolated, but still a woman replete, laden with gifts, musical, athletic, clever as a general, and seems to sit before me, even now, when she is gone,

gone for ever, as real as though I could reach forward and touch her, so powerful, so completely present, and so lovely.

'But it's spring now,' she said, as if this had been the sum of her difficulty in speaking.

'It's early spring,' I said. 'We could be married in April.'

I had no idea what she was thinking then. She certainly didn't say. Had she intended to go back to England and resume her teaching? Or join her brother in his practice in Roscommon?

I suddenly felt this was a hand I could not win. I could see the horses massing at the starting gates, they were under starter's orders, they were off, and my poor nag was surely that broken-backed creature toiling at the rear, falling away at every stride, the loser not only of the race but of every furlong of it. A pit of misery opened its trap door under me. I knew it, I knew it, I was going to lose her. My confidence ludicrously misplaced. Her vulnerability laughably misdiagnosed.

'Alright,' she said.

Like a jolt of electricity.

'I'm sorry if I seem sad,' she said, looking at me, smiling, 'I can't seem to help it. You're so kind to me, Jack. And I do love you.'

'April then,' I said, laughing.

'April,' she said.

———

'Marry for love,' Pappy used to say when we were children, 'or you'll live your life on Standalone Point and be buried in Melancholy Lane.' These were actual places in Sligo, one a sandy spit jutting out onto the sloblands of the Garvoge river, the other somewhere in the eastern end of town.

Chapter Eight

Just as night fell, I had two visitors, an officer and a constable of the transitional police force – so, I suppose, in
being between two things, suitable people to appear in
the twilight. One was a whiteman, sweating profusely,
but a handsome individual all the same, the other one
of those very severe-looking, very dark-skinned lads,
mostly Nigerians, that dominate the rank and file. Just
like in the old days in Ireland, when Eneas would be
posted anywhere but his native Sligo, they prefer to have
strangers policing strangers, because a local man will
have too many ties among his own people.

The 'new' police don't have a particularly good name
in Accra, certainly not in Tom Quaye's reckoning, and
indeed he was just leaving as they arrived, and I watched
the three of them from the porch window, talking for a
few moments on the dry dust of the compound, Tom's
attitude and angle of body speaking eloquently of reluctance and fear.

The black constable at any rate was plain and forth-
right in his roughness and hostility, and it appeared
Tom was now obliged to return to the house in their

company, because in he came, quite apologetically, trailing the policemen.

'These two men are here talking to you, major,' he said.

'Well,' I said.

The white officer strode in just as a visiting friend might, at his ease, master of the moment. He enjoyed the rank of inspector, to judge by his cap insignia.

'McNulty?' he said. 'J. C. McNulty?'

'That's right,' I said.

'A few questions, if I may,' he said. I was thinking his accent was Irish, but North of the border, Belfast maybe.

'Of course,' I said. 'Will I ask Tom to make some tea for us?'

The inspector didn't look at his constable but declined for both of them. He waved me into one of my own cane chairs, then seated himself opposite on the chair I usually reserve for my feet. The constable stayed looming where he was, and Tom hovered at the door, hoping for a quick dismissal.

'So what brings you to see me, inspector?' I said.

Before the inspector could answer, the constable suddenly spoke very fast and confidently to Tom in what must have been Hausa, not Ewe at any rate. Tom replied with one brief syllable, which might have been yes or no, I couldn't say.

'The constable is just establishing that your house-boy was in your company when the fracas occurred,' said the inspector. He had shaved with perfect meticulousness except for a miniature moustache just under his nostrils where the razor hadn't been able to reach, due to the overhang of his nose.

'What fracas?'

'The fracas which occurred in Osu on Friday night.'

'I don't honestly recall any fracas,' I said.

'Perhaps you recall that a man, Kofi Genfi, was injured?'

'No.' I was genuinely surprised, but at the same time, playing back through my muddled memories of the evening, there did seem to be some mysterious elements floating about, such as me being sat on, or something of the kind. And then there was the equally vague memory of my amorousness.

'We are questioning everyone who attended, but in particular the group you were in. You caused quite a stir apparently. Are you in the habit of going dancing with your houseboy?'

'No,' I said.

'I was especially hoping you would remember the incident. The people here are not as a rule inclined to be open with us but I thought that as a European you might be more obliging.'

'I'm afraid the truth is I was very drunk.'

Thus far he didn't seem to mind any of my answers, one way or another. He remained perfectly affable. A very good policeman I thought. I had no way of knowing what he was thinking.

'Your full name is John Charles McNulty, is it not? You were in the sappers in the war and subsequently were with the UN here and in Togoland?'

'Yes. Here in Accra, mostly.'

'But you were in Togo, were you not, during the time of the plebiscite?'

'Yes, I was.'

'And what keeps you here in Accra, Mr McNulty?'

What indeed?

'I am just – pausing, I think, before I go back to Ireland. I am writing a little,' I said, regretting saying it, but at the same time unexpectedly proud of my strange activity.

'Oh?' he said.

I waved towards the table, and the discarded minute-book, as if that said everything that needed to be said.

'May I take a look?' he said. And before I could say yea or nay in any language, he scraped back his chair and went over to the table and took up this book. He opened it and for some reason read aloud the first sentence he saw there, random, and mysterious: '*When I started to bring her almost weekly to the cinema in Galway I realised the pictures were something of a religion for her –* I don't understand,' he said.

'It's just a sort of memoir, I suppose,' I said, as embarrassed now as I had been proud. 'My wife died some years ago. It is a memoir about her, I suppose. Jottings.'

'Do you think I could take it?' he said.

'It's just a personal, very personal account of things. It has no relevance to anyone except myself, and even then, I am not sure why I am writing it. By the way, I didn't catch your name.'

He was still scanning through the pages.

'Is it a diary?' he said.

'No, I don't believe so. I didn't catch your name, inspector.'

He seemed to have become briefly deaf. I devoutly did not wish him to take the book away. I knew if he took it away I would not be able to go on with it, illogical as that was.

But much to my relief he seemed to lose interest in the book, and placed it back down where he had found it, and returned to the chair. Then he sat for a half-minute saying nothing, but looking at me quietly.

'What was interesting to us when your name came up was not that you were drinking in Osu, or even that Mr Genfi was so badly injured. It was that, when I brought your name to Mr Oko, your landlord, and he spoke of your service in the UN, I contacted them, and was told the reason you were let go.'

He let this sink in a little, and I smiled, not knowing what else to do.

'Do you want to say anything about that?' he said.

'I think there might be a certain confidentiality attached to it,' I said.

I felt I knew now what was coming. That unpleasantness in Ho was going to haunt me. The Swede, Emmanuel Heyst, and his mad schemes. I had been duped by him, and his promises of easy money. There is no such thing.

'Oh?' he said. 'Gunrunning, wasn't it? Do you see, Ghana is still a volatile entity as I'm sure you appreciate. Certain aspects of things still festering . . . And we are very interested in the reason you have remained here in Accra, with this implication hanging over you of gunrunning in the past.' Then he said, in the next breath, as if the two things were connected, 'You might be amused to know that I served for some years in the Ulster Constabulary. There is a long association between Ireland and the police force here, in one form or another.'

'Oh?' I said.

Gunrunning. That word ringing in my ears.

'Well, what may one say about that?' he said, smiling.

'About what?'

'Your activities.'

'There were no activities. It was a misunderstanding.

There is no record of me gunrunning in Togo or anywhere else. The official in the UN was quite wrong to say so. I was friendly with a man there, a Swede, who did indeed turn out to be supplying guns to rebels, rebels who, I may add, never had occasion to rebel, in the upshot, because the plebiscite was successful. And the Swede, Emmanuel Heyst, as I am sure you know, was arrested and prosecuted.'

'He was, of course, yes,' said the inspector. Then he stood up. 'This visit is by way of warning. Do you understand? I didn't come through Ireland and Palestine only to be fucked around by the likes of you.'

I could only look at him quizzically, neutrally.

'If we were to find that you were engaged in a similar activity – and if you are it will come to light, as sure as night follows day – we would bring the full force of the law down on you, and you will be dealt with definitively and thoroughly.'

Now he was not so calm, or calm in a different way, rather austere and proud-looking, like the matador driving in his thin sword.

'You are not an entirely desirable person here. My advice to you would be to go home as soon as you can. You have absolutely no role to play here in Ghana. If you are up to no good, you will find you have made a terrible mistake in thinking you could get away with it.'

He had made his point, and knew it. I was filled suddenly with foreboding and misery. Not just because of what he had said. Something less concrete, something deep under everything, some alteration in the ground of myself, a little earthquake. Why *had* I stayed in Accra? Why was I here, with Tom, on the wrong side of the Atlantic Ocean? It was the question I had not been able to answer, and having been asked it again by this policeman, still could find no answer, for him or for me.

'Well,' he said. 'Good evening.'

I nodded to him, not able to find a decent response. The constable, who of course had not said a word to me throughout but had stood there looking as fierce as a Malay god, followed his inspector out into the full darkness of the night.

I just sat there for a while, and Tom stayed where he was too.

'Policemen are not good people,' he said then.

'What happened to Genfi,' I said, 'this Kofi Genfi?'

'You kissed his woman and you had a fight and then he sat on you and then someone pulled him off because he was wanting to kill you and then he went out to kill his woman and her brother stopped him with a great blow and he is in the hospital.'

'This is why I swore off drinking, this is why I will never drink again.'

'It was these policemen killed my friends during the veterans' march. Arrested us, and tortured us. They say it is a different force but they are the same.'

'Never, never again, so help me God.'

'Amen,' said Tom.

Chapter Nine

1926. Our marriage. On the one side of the church, the rather elegant and choice individuals who had travelled to see Mai wed, her aunt Maria Sheridan from Cavan, the one with the connection to Collins, encased in a brocaded day dress, giving her a slightly ironclad look, but very smart. Mai's other aunts from Roscommon, Cavan and Leitrim, glinting in the holy gloom of the chapel, with small dots of gold and ruby light playing on old rings and necklaces and bracelets. And chief before all, her resplendent brother, Jack, the doctor from Roscommon, lofty, silk-hatted, confident, and silent. He was a man Mai adored, and he was said to adore her, even if he was a rare visitor, being devoted to fishing the rivers of Roscommon, and shooting at the wildlife there. He was six foot six in his stockings, I knew, and in every way he was as impressive to me as her father had been, and I prayed he would approve of me.

All of these souls sitting on their side with the easy, rather solemn, occupying air that in other circumstances would have put me in suspicion that they were actually Protestants.

On the other side, my side, my very dapper brother Tom, in his best suit, tailored by my father of course, and no tailor in Dublin could have made a better one, even if it was a few years out of date, strictly speaking, but, if he looked provincial, nevertheless it was provincial with a touch of pleasing swagger about it. Then there was my father, Old Tom, who had decided to retrieve a straw boater from some dark corner of his bedroom. And he had fashioned for himself a set of tails and black trousers, to some degree let down by an old grey coat, an item he never attempted as a tailor, and so was shop-bought. He sat very still on the pew, with his eyes closed, so that he looked like one of those old photographs of executed train robbers in America, put out somewhere as a warning to the frontier populace.

Beside him sat my mother and something in the day had undone her intentions somewhat because it is probably true to say that her attire was not quite right. She wore her old cloth hat and her plain, black, severe little dress that, unlike Maria Sheridan's, which was also severe, had not cost too much in the first place, because my mother didn't care about such things.

Mai herself, then, coming in on the arm of Nicholas Sheridan, Maria's husband, in her wedding dress, a long brushmark of silk.

Now I was beside Mai, staring forward at the priest. He spoke the question to me, and I answered him, 'I do,' he fixing me with his eyes, keeping my eyes on his with a fierce effort, as if for a crazy moment I were marrying him, and then he put the same question to Mai, and there was a silence, that begged to be filled with her voice, with her assenting, and yet there was nothing, I hardly dared look sideways at her, now I was getting a little angry, angry at this bloody silence, you wouldn't treat a dog like that, a man in a wedding suit tailored by his own father, with a fine little buttonhole, my mother's face now in the furthest reach of my sight whitened by fright, as perhaps my own was – 'I do,' she said.

We signed the Register of Marriages in the porch of the church, a huddle of varied souls, my mother, elated, on the edge of dancing, you might think, my father smiling and innocently pleased, the boater knocked back on his head. He shook Mai's hand with fervour after she signed her name beside my own in the old book, and she kissed him on the cheek, leaning down to him a little. Then she kissed my mother and her own many aunts and cousins. Then her brother shook my hand and I thanked him for his kind offices of the day. There was a moment of peace. All was right, everything in its place, a consummation so far of my life, the logical and just outcome of my love for Mai. It was Nicholas who had paid for the little reception in the Great Southern Hotel, and it was my mother had put together the stupendous cake. It was Tom who had bought the train tickets to Dublin and arranged the few nights in Barry's Hotel. The priest, having finished his performance, had all the ease of the actor released from his work. The rainy light, shouldering into the porch from the great door, seemed the light of goodness and promise.

Mai was gone so quickly that when I went out into the narrow street there was no sign of her. But down beside the old church was her veil, like a spider's web cleaned out of God's mansion, that gave all the signs of having been wrenched from her head and discarded. It was pelting with rain and I had no coat, but I thought if I made a dash along Buttermilk Walk I might catch her. As I rounded the corner into St Augustine Street, a little girl was standing there, looking at the palm of her hand, where I could see a gold band, Mai's wedding ring. Fifty yards along was Mai, a white ghost in the sheeting rain, hurrying away towards the river.

In the distance the rain was dropping in dozens of huge, grey curtains, frittered and torn, across the vista of small houses. Although it was early afternoon, there was a darkness everywhere caused by the very solidity of the countless raindrops. In the midst of this, like a pulsing white heart, was Mai's diminishing figure.

She will be crossing Wolfe Tone Bridge in a second, I thought. Then she would be scudding along the edge of the Claddagh. Where was she going? What was she thinking of? I crossed the bridge in her wake, I skirted along the Claddagh, keeping her within view. The spring tide had risen and the sea wind was noisily throwing the tide at the dry-harbours and sea-walls, so that spouts of water were pirouetting and twisting into the air, drenching anyone who passed. Now I reached the Grattan Road, where the violent-looking sea crowded the bay, it looked like.

There she was, my new wife, still fifty yards ahead. Now the storm decided it wasn't doing enough and started to roar and howl. Only a few years previously I had followed her along this very road, as she went home from the college. I had known nothing about her then. Did I know much more now? At the surface of things perhaps I was embarrassed, not in any way knowing what I would say to our wedding guests, but deeper somewhere I was moved by a wild concern for her, as if it wasn't me she was fleeing from, and I was only the observer of this strange emergency.

The barracks where the Black and Tans used to be stationed passed on my right, as gloomy and as derelict as the history it remembered or forgot. Indeed I recalled Mr Kirwan inveighing against their one-time presence there 'in an innocent Irish seaside place'. Finally I reached the turn of the Grattan Road that brought a traveller round to the front of the houses. I could see poor Grattan House huddled in the rain, like a forlorn image of the vanished Mr Kirwan, his times and hours all done.

Now I got to the handsome old gates and looked in through the bars. Much to my relief, there she was, inside the porch itself, in rather a strange position, her right hand grasping the door-knocker but no longer banging on it, if she had been banging on it, and her body hanging from this arm, her head lain sideways on her left shoulder, and the torso and legs slumping. Her face was resting it looked like against the neglected paint of the front door. I slipped in and walked quietly up to her. I could have been angry I suppose. I could have railed and accused, but in truth I felt for her only an unexpected respect.

'Mai,' I said. I fancied I could hear her breathing heavily. Black clouds went racing high above the cold roof of the house. All the prettiness and the desirability seemed to have gone out of it. I was surprised that her brother Jack, to whom the house was left, had let it go, but of course he lived in Roscommon where his practice was. There was a bloom of spring grass across the once pristine gravel. Because the tide was high, the callows field beside the house was brimming with dark water, and only the brown stalks of last year's ragwort showed above the waterline. It was such a melancholy sight.

'He's not here,' she said then. 'He's not here.'

'There's no one here, Mai,' I said.

'I thought maybe Pappy would be here but he's not.'

'Your father, you remember, Mai, your father is gone.'

'I know,' she said.

Then she straightened and turned herself about. I never saw a human person so utterly drenched unless it was a swimmer. Her lovely wedding dress looked like white seaweed on her, clinging everywhere.

'Jesus, Mary, and St Joseph,' I said.

'I know,' she said.

'Is this it, Mai? Do you not want to be married to me? Is that what it is?'

'I took fright,' she said. 'I took fright.'

'At what, at what?'

'I don't know. I took fright.'

She lifted her face and looked at me.

'There's nothing to be frightened of,' I said, but wondered if that were true.

'Do you think we could get in through a window?' she said. 'I would love to see the old place again.'

'It's not in a fit state,' I said, stepping to the parlour window, where I had sometimes knocked to get her mother's attention. I was intending to try and peer in. But it was only a subterfuge. As soon as I moved away, she was gone, moving at speed to the garden wall, and was over it swiftly, and splashed down into the flooded field. She waded twenty feet out towards God knew what limit of the ground, where surely she would imminently plunge underwater and be lost. I cleared the wall myself and sloshed along in the murky floodwaters, trying to catch up with her, alarmed by the darkness of everything, the indistinctness. Then she stopped and I came up behind her. I saw her shoulders fall. I could hear her crying, a sound I don't think I had ever heard from her before. Her crying was oddly deep, and I was horribly affrighted by it.

'I want to go back,' she said.

'You want to go back where?'

'I want to go back, I want to go back,' she said.

'I don't understand,' I said.

I stepped closer to her and put my two hands on her hips either side, and then when she made no obvious objection, put my arms around her, and stood as close to her as I could. I was fearful of knocking her over, on the rough ground beneath us. It was very surprising that, soaked as she was, coatless and hatless, in the vicious storm, her body under the silk was as warm as a running engine.

'I gave my wedding ring to a little beggar girl.'

'I got it back,' I said, 'I gave her a shilling for it.'

'Poor little mite of a thing she was.'

There was no difficulty after all explaining things to the wedding guests. They were puzzled I am sure, but amused, and put it all down to Mai's high-spirited nature. Maria Sheridan said it was the most romantic thing she had ever heard, how I had followed her into the water. Maria was very close to Mai, it seemed, and intended to leave her her property in Cavan when she and Nicholas 'went to a better place', as she put it. So whatever Maria said was gospel, I supposed. It was just Mai's high-spirited nature. Her brother Jack prescribed her a calming powder and made sure she had not caught her death. The soaking clothes were taken off her by Maria and my mother, and in the corridor while I waited I heard their laughter now in the hotel room.

Then we had the nicest honeymoon. Mai loved Dublin. Every afternoon we went to the pictures, and in the evenings to a concert. Mai's favourite composer was Purcell, and we saw *Dido and Aeneas* at the Antient Concert Rooms. How often I have heard Mai humming that to herself. 'Dido's Lament'. She was gracious about the shortcomings of Barry's Hotel, and later wrote a nice note about it to Tom, thanking him. She seemed a different woman now in Dublin, certain and vigorous. She linked me in the streets confidently, she told me long stories about her youth in Salthill and her adventures teaching in England. It was suddenly as if our marriage was a shell on the stormy sea from which she was going to step, Venus renewed, ready for her second life. We made love to each other in the dowdy hotel room with the unfakeable and ineradicable happiness of ordinary lovers.

> *When I am laid in earth*
> *May my wrongs create*
> *No trouble in thy breast –*
> *Remember me, forget my fate.*

Chapter Ten

For the last two weeks, the mosquitoes having had their wicked way with me, I have suffered the inevitable outcome. The first I knew of it, I awoke feeling as if I had drunk a jar of spoiled potín, though I hadn't touched a drop of anything since the night of the fracas – the night indeed when the mosquitoes ravaged me. A tide of nausea and fever poured through me, saturating everything in sweat. I could neither rise nor stay comfortably where I was. My mother came to my bedside in ghostly ministration and soothed my brow, an unlikely visitation in every respect, including the fact that she was standing on the side of my bed where it abuts the solid wall, or what passes for a solid wall here in Oiswe Street. She smiled at me and then melted away. An enormous sorrow assailed me, only rubbed out by fits of coughing, bullying coughing. When Tom Quaye finally came in to work, he found his employer with his arms outstretched like a petty Jesus, chest heaving, and his head a small boulder struck again and again by a lump hammer.

Tom hurried away to fetch the doctor but he knew immediately, as I did myself, that it was malaria. I've had malaria many times, but the chaos and the storm of it always surprises me. A man forgets the experience of malaria. Mai said if a woman could really remember the experience of childbirth she would never have another baby. With a proper memory of malaria no man would ever abide in Africa.

Tom brought back a doctor from the town, a Dr Christiansen, a big blockhouse of a Dane with a hearty laugh and a merciless manner. I don't remember what I said to him in those first days. I don't remember much of anything. There was a lot of to-ing and fro-ing of people, but apart from Tom and the doctor, none of these was real, I suppose. Mai did not make an entrance, though in my deepest delirium I seem to remember calling out to her. Maybe it was best she did not come. It would have been so strange.

Actually while I lay suffering we did have a visitor of real flesh and blood, but I don't remember him either. Apparently, according to Tom, it was Kofi Genfi's assailant, his second assailant shall we say, the brother of his beautiful woman, asking for money. It seems the police have closed their investigation, and now this other man feels emboldened or perhaps obliged to seek compensation for his victim, which is rather odd and complicated, and Tom struggled even with his excellent English to explain it to me. The fact that it was he himself who decked his sister's lover is not as relevant as I would have first thought, except maybe as an added encouragement to come all the way out to me here, in so far as I imagine he must be feeling guilty about it. But in his eyes, the man believes he did me a good turn, in preventing a murder, or even a double murder, of the woman and of me. The main gist of it was, however, that he wanted money to give to Kofi Genfi, who has been impoverished by his stay in hospital, which Tom tells me is ruinously expensive for a Ghanaian. Kofi Genfi received a felling blow to the side of the head, and is having difficulty going about his usual tasks, not to mention a broken arm that is healing badly. I think Tom was delicately implying that I might have been responsible for the arm.

'Well, Tom,' I said, 'what did you say to him? Do you think I should pay something towards Mr Genfi's costs?'

'No, major, you should not. He is not a good man. He was many times in prison. He is a violent man. *Krezy!* Once you give a man like that a shilling he will be back every day for a pound. Mark my words,' said Tom, with his nice use of phrases.

I found this immensely reassuring, because up to that point, all the while he had been talking I had been under the heavy premonition of being touched for money by Tom himself, which would have made me very sorrowful. Now his certainty and wisdom encouraged me. Moreover, he had nursed me through the floodtide of the sickness, his large arms lifting me to the latrine again and again, and mopping up vomit and whatnot with the indifferent will of a mother. Every night for the two weeks I knew he had sat out in the front room with my table and jottings, the cane chair pulled to the wall, because he liked to lean it back and balance on the back legs. As I came out of my fever I had heard him softly singing there, and telling o'er and o'er the secret beads of his own private concerns. I am deeply in his debt and indeed might well have been content to hand over a few quid to help Mr Genfi. But Tom would have none of that.

'I hope this man understood the situation, Tom, when you had explained there would be no money?'

'Ah,' said Tom, and left it there, as if he didn't wish to venture a lie about such a matter, or any opinion at all. Then he went off to the kitchen and brewed up some tea. Dr Christiansen had put me to the expense of various bought medicines, and Tom had dutifully doled these out to me, spoon by spoon, and pill by pill. Maybe he didn't think Aunty-aunty was the woman for malaria itself, even if her remedy for the bites had been very effective.

We rented a few rooms in a battered old mansion in Galway and gathered a few sticks about us, and called ourselves proper married people.

A month hadn't passed before we got the famous tele-gram from Maria Sheridan, 'mayfly up', and we were excited to drive ourselves eastwards to Omard, to show ourselves off there as a newly married couple.

Omard House was a lodestar of welcome, and Mai had often talked about it. The Sheridans had no chil-dren of their own and it had always been intimated that Mai as their favourite niece would inherit Omard – an exciting thing to contemplate. When the yellow wings of the mayfly clogged the air above Lough Sheelin, this was the much longed-for signal for Maria's friends and family to drop everything and set out to Cavan. And Nicholas's brother Felix, not the full shilling, but a harmless soul, would faithfully sweep the leaves and the debris of winter off the tennis court, and mend the old dam in the stream that came down from the mountains, so a salmon-pool there would deepen for the swimming. And the parish priest, the doctor, the solicitor, and the bank manager, and sundry strong Catholic farmers from round about, and all the aunts and cousins, would con-verge on the old house as if they too were a species of mayfly, obeying an immemorial call.

Mai's brother, Jack, with his atmosphere of silence and his preternatural height, was already there when we arrived, having hurried over from Roscommon with his fishing rods and his reels. Coming into the old hall I was relieved when he came forward and shook my hand.

'There now,' he said, and I don't think he uttered much more than that the whole visit.

As Mai's husband, I was welcomed, I felt the special honour of it. At the long kitchen table heaped with the fruits of the farm, we took our places not just as guests but as guests delighted in – Maria plainly adored the presence of these living souls she had chosen to be in her house.

Mai fearlessly played the piano in the evening. During the day on the tennis court she destroyed opponents, young and old. In her one-piece bathing suit of darkest blue, she swam in confident circles about the salmon-pool, her cousin Felix laughing in his daft way as he watched her. Secure in Maria's regard, and rejoicing in it, I talked to her about my travels, which she seemed to like, and to her husband Nicholas, a former Justice of the Peace under the old regime, and that rare bird, a Catholic landlord, about bridges, roads and ditches, the three points we had in common.

In 1920 Omard had sheltered Michael Collins's fiancée, Kitty Kiernan. Collins of course by the time of our first visit was dead. But during the war of independence he had come down to Cavan on election business, and became friends with the Kiernans, who ran a little hotel in Granard, and a general store. One day a police inspector from Dublin was shot dead while he was drinking at the hotel bar. The Kiernans were friendly with that young policeman, and yet also friends with Collins – the two opposing parties, as we would say in the UN, of the conflict. And most likely the inspector was killed by associates of Collins. But whatever about the Irish complexities of the situation, nine lorry-loads of RIC policemen and soldiers from the barracks in Cavan came into the town and torched the Kiernan properties in reprisal, and most of Granard into the bargain. The Kiernans themselves, including Kitty, fled to Omard, where the Sheridans sheltered them, earning I am sure the gratitude of Collins in those uncertain times.

The rooks complained mightily in the beech trees, the twilight lost heart under the branches, and the tennis players played on into the darkness, mad to win. Jack Kirwan came back from the river with his sticks of dangling trout, old Felix raved in the avenues, and Maria stoked the fires in the rooms, and boiled up great pots of spuds, and roasted and baked and broiled, and the sense of things going forward steady and right was palpable and inspiring.

I was proud, very proud to be among such people, and be accepted by them. I was introduced to the lights and luminaries of Kilnaleck as 'Jack McNulty, Mai Kirwan's husband, a young civil engineer' – as if they were a string of noble titles.

Our days in Africa, days of our youth, unrepeatable, beyond price.

At first she wasn't sure she wanted to go out, in the service, as it were, of the British.

I crossed to London for my interview at the Foreign Office. There was a very nice gentleman there, who was surprisingly encouraged by the fact that I had only a second-class degree. He said the best sort of man for the colonies was not your first-class honours man, all push and polish, but a resourceful, second-class sort. I was offered a post in the Gold Coast, what they used to call the Whiteman's Grave. I didn't tell Mai that.

But if I go back thirty years to 1927, when we came out together, I wonder to what degree I can step back into a realm that is real? The colonial life around me then for the first time, the bright, expanded world that it seemed, lent that present time as I lived it a curious, heightened quality.

I seem to see Mai clearly nonetheless, in the startling guise of her youth. Her hair has not submitted to the African light, her skin has not surrendered to the African heat, like the wives of old Jack Reynolds and Billy Ketchum, the two other colonial officers in our station. Her beautiful ease with everyone is evident, resulting in her being liked by everyone, sometimes extravagantly, in particular Mrs Reynolds and Mrs Ketchum, both of whom had daughters of Mai's age, but far away in England. Mai was not a drinking woman like they were, though she delighted in the cherries from their cocktails, which they fed her like you might a special pet.

'Dear Mrs McNulty' they called her, as if 'dear' were a sort of honorary title, and even when she wasn't in their company, I would hear them referring to her, sitting perhaps in the shade of the baobab trees, as 'dear Mrs McNulty' this, and 'dear Mrs McNulty' that.

We had reached the station, initially, after what she had called 'rather interesting hardship'. Our means of transport was a small, sand-filled, boiling bus going down across the Sahara between North Africa and the Gold Coast. It had once been painted, but a dozen sandstorms had stripped it back to the metal. The desert was as big as Europe. Humanity, local and imperial, milled about the oases, scorning the heat in mysterious displays of intent. Then these would drop away, and the wide, soul-emptying desert begin again, in which the bus was only a loudmouthed intruder.

Inside the bus, in its jacket of burning metal, sat myself and Mai, she gazing out at this increasing distance between herself and civilisation, and myself gazing at her when she wasn't looking, worrying about her opinion of Africa, and her opinion of me bringing her there.

But as I watched her, there was sometimes a look of pure gaiety on her face, whether from thinking her own thoughts, or because something she had seen had pleased her, though what there was in the vast, repeated sameness of the desert I didn't know. With my degree in geology I knew what sort of ground we drove over. I could guess the history of the sand grains, and know what rocks were folded into others, and could visualise the ancient forests and seas that would once have graced that place. I knew all that but little enough about the geology of my new wife.

But Mai was excited by the colonial life, all in all. Our station was tiny, remote, but neatly composed. She liked me in my white uniforms, she liked the mud-walled bungalow with its big rooms, she liked the order of things, what she called the Britishness, and the deference shown to her by everyone. She put her old politics aside, and looked about her, in a widened and interested way. She read books about the tribes of the Gold Coast, the languages, the jewellery and furniture, the chieftains, and the witch doctors.

She burned with presence, just as the country burned with its incessant heat. She was young, and she didn't betray the gift of her youth. She seemed to know damn well the privilege of it, and luxuriated in it.

In the evenings, as if Africa were an extended Omard, she played the piano for us, the Ketchums, the Reynolds, and myself. One evening she played a tremendous piece of Chopin, sight unseen. Mai's face was fiercely concentrated, her eyes seemingly boring into the sheet music, until you might have feared small black marks would appear there and burst into flames. The women listened with their habitual wonder to this Irishwoman whose gifts seemed so abundant. Jack and Billy, benignly leaning against the club bar, seemed also to be touched by Mai's playing, she hitting the keys at the end in a terrific chord, making Mrs Reynolds and Mrs Ketchum jump in their wicker seats.

'That was just so marvellous, dear Mrs McNulty,' Mrs Ketchum said.

Then Mai suggested I sing 'Roses of Picardy', the song she had now often heard me singing while I shaved.

'Well, I will if you want me to, Mai. But I can't compete with your playing.'

'Go on, Jack,' she said, 'to please me.'

'Of course I will sing to please you,' I said.

'I should think so,' said Jack Reynolds, drily.

And the roses will die in the summertime,
And our paths may be far apart,
But there's one rose that dies not in Picardy,
'Tis the rose that I keep in my heart.

'Jolly well done, Jack, jolly well done,' Billy Ketchum said, tearfully, at the end, a man after all who had come through the Picardy in question.

Chapter Eleven

Mai ordered a rake of books about obstetrics and set about establishing a little clinic at the station, not for the likes of us, but the native wives and children. There was a high incidence of puerperal fever among newborn babies and Mai began to teach the mothers about the importance of scrupulous cleanliness. These were in no way savage people, and they listened to her, with our houseboy Tom Nobody translating for her.

Tom Nobody, I had nearly forgotten him. The first Tom, before Tom Quaye. When he had been told at school to take an English name he had chosen Nobody because he liked the sound of the word. Mai and Tom mutually approved of each other. She was anxious that he be well dressed, and she had two white suits made up for him, and supplied him with a proper cork hat. As a matter of fact she didn't contribute to those continuous and desultory conversations about the natives. Mrs Ketchum and Mrs Reynolds would routinely boil over with scorn for the African, and for Africa. Billy Ketchum might start to complain about 'the stench in the villages'. Then Mai was silent, mysterious, with her Sphinx-like smile.

If there were no savage tribes to subdue, she certainly subdued Thomas, Lord Goodworth, the governor in Accra – Goody to his friends. He found the funds for her. It was unpaid work, and unofficial, apart from his good offices. She had, it turned out, dollops and dashes of medical knowledge from her brother Jack, and every month Dr Booth made his way up from Accra with supplies and held his surgery and she dreamed of getting Queenie Moran out to be the nurse in the small wooden building, though that never came to pass. In that way she earned herself the legend of something of a miracle worker, and the death rate fell to nearly nothing. Mrs Kétchum marvelled at the fact that the heat did not seem to trouble Mai in the least. She went about the burning compound without umbrella or hat, and was quite content to be so tanned she might have passed for an Arab woman. One morning early I awoke, and turned to look at her in the bed. The sheet had been kicked away in the darkness, and now her long white body lay there, with the darkened face, and the arms brown to the elbows. Her body innocent and eternal, like in an old painting.

By then, married for three years, I sometimes worried that she might be growing tired of me. You have to worry about something. But it was a worry that waxed and waned. As district officer I was often away on tour, and then I could imagine all sorts of things, worrying myself as I lay uncomfortably on my camp bed, but when I was at home I realised afresh that life in the colonies suited her. Nothing so confining, you might think, as to be one of only three white women for a thousand miles, in the great, weather-afflicted, unwalkable spaces of West Africa. But no, she liked that. There was sometimes a sense of 'inspection' from her. We would sit in the evenings in the bungalow on our cane chairs, and if I was reading Tennyson or Kipling, drinking whisky slowly, the moths burning themselves to death on the Tilley lamps, she was sometimes simply watching me, and it was not always a completely comfortable feeling. She said little enough in that mood, but now and then after a long silence she might make a comment, as if in answer to a companion I couldn't see or hear. Oftentimes she took me by surprise, commenting on some aspect of things that had never occurred to me.

'Do you know,' she said once, 'in a hundred years, the Africans might be in charge of us. I hope they'll forgive us.'

'What do you mean, Mai?' I said.

'Oh,' she said, 'we've got used to having the power of life and death over people. Do you know Billy Ketchum hanged a man here last year? Oh, yes,' she said, 'that sort of thing tends to see-saw back and forth.'

'No, Mai, I don't think so. No.'

'Trust me, Jack.'

'Well, we mightn't be alive to see it.'

'Just as well, Jack, you being a district officer and all.'

Then she had the good grace to laugh.

'I'm not blaming *you*, Jack. I like you. I will definitely step in and stop them when they try to hang you.'

'Thank you, Mai.'

The plain fact is, I was delighted to sit there with her, whatever she said, whatever she was thinking. I was proud of her. I thought, no, I knew, that she was a wonderful and unique woman. Unusual was the unkindest adjective you could have used about her. She was unusual. Her allure for me anyway was boundless.

Even last night I had a vivid dream where she was being 'kind' to me, as she called it – 'Now I'll be kind,' she would say – listening to me speaking with a slightly ironical attention, doing her level best, and not making that little snorting noise, and when I paused in my speech – I can't remember what I was saying – she moved nearer to me and put her arms around my shoulders. Then she shifted just an inch closer. It was the barest movement, and yet in my dream it crushed the breath from me.

Then she was obliged to head homeward. She was pregnant.

'It must be catching,' she said. 'All those healthy young babies in the clinic.'

However, Dr Booth and the ladies of the station advised her to go back to Europe. Alas, I had six months of my contract to run. So off she would have to go, alone, indomitable, with her leather cases, and one black sea-trunk marked in white letters:

Mrs Mai McNulty,

c/o Mrs Thomas McNulty,

John Street, Sligo, Irish Free State.

Not Wanted on the Voyage.

'You'll be sure and take care of yourself, Mai,' I said.

'Don't worry, Jack. I think I know what's involved. Don't be late for the christening.'

'Oh, Mai,' I said, 'Mai. What a turn-up for the books. A child. I'm so bloody happy.'

'Yes,' she said, 'yes, you're right,' she said, veritably beaming. 'It's a good thing alright. I think I'm supposed to say well done to you. Or is that just what men say to each other?'

'You can say well done if you like.'

'I will then. Well done.'

'Well done, you, Mai.'

'Ah, yes, sure, yes, I had to make a great effort, I must say.'

'You're a horrible woman,' I said, laughing.

'I know,' she said. 'Horrible.'

She had recently rescued an orphaned Diana monkey, so she decided to take him with her.

'At last,' she said, 'a decent conversationalist.'

'Well, well,' I said.

'I will miss you, Jack, though,' she said, in her serious voice.

'Will you?'

'God, yes,' she said.

Mrs Ketchum and Mrs Reynolds came out to say their goodbyes, all handkerchiefs and genuine sorrow, and promises to visit her one day in Ireland. She was given a send-off by the women of the village, which pleased her greatly, and an ivory elephant to remember her time in Africa.

I travelled down with her as far as the sea and entrusted her to the long looming ship of the Peninsular and Orient line. In the car she had taken my left hand between gear changes, and once or twice had laid it on her stomach. She was shaking going up the gangplank. A liner like that makes everyone look small at the rail.

While she was aboard ship on the long journey, I had to go higher up in Asante country, checking on the progress of a new canal.

There were the sweltering hours of work to endure, while I paced among the diggers, as we tried to extend the supply of water northward. The ruling chiefs had requested a canal and the Colonial Office had obliged. It was a noble exercise, and my heart would normally have been in it. But my heart on this occasion had slipped away with Mai.

My mother came all the way up from Sligo to Dublin to meet her. Mai stepped off the boat at the North Wall, and there was the Mam, in her old black dress, faithfully attending. Mai said my mother wanted to hold her hand along the quay, as if she were a child, but because Mai was tall enough and my mother so diminutive, it was the older woman who gave at a glance the appearance of youth. And anyway Mai was not sure she wished for her hand to be taken, she in her capacious dark blue coat that she had bought while the ship docked at Gibraltar, to hide her condition, the monkey like a black and white flame tinged with orange on her shoulder. She was grateful to my mother for coming to meet her, but she didn't want to be treated like an invalid. But my mother persisted, and led Mai all the way to the train at Kingsbridge, and fussed over her every inch of the journey to Sligo.

She was to have the baby in the little house in John Street. She didn't think it would be feasible for her brother in Roscommon to take her, even though he was a doctor. Maria Sheridan said she would be glad to receive her in Omard, but Mai was not that sure, as if somehow or other a pregnancy was something beyond the scope of a visit to Omard. John Street was hardly big enough to swing a cat, let alone a Diana monkey, but Mai preferred to be there.

꙳

The rains, finally. All day there had been a metallic grey-ness at the edges of the usual egg-blue sky. A few minutes ago the universe gave a shrug, time seemed to step back, then surged forward to catch up, and then the heavens were ripped in a thousand places like a rotten topsail. And a solid water poured down, you might think no creature could breathe in it. It rubbed out every other sound, of insect, bird and animal. The palm trees dipped under it like dancers, their lovely costumes dragged and battered. The iron roof was betrayed, a dozen holes immediately found out where they had grown unnoticed. I had to rush to move my table down a few feet as the pages of the minute-book were splattered with a dusty grey blood, it looked like. It was so alive, the rain, that I laughed out loud. Tom stood by my side watching it, forcefully cursing the deluge. He knew it might be making a hames of his shelter, over in the big-leaved trees.

I looked at him. Though his eyes are hooded and nearly hidden, yet out through the folds of skin shine two slivers of emerald. I don't know how sad he is, but I do know that he is sad. He has been extraordinarily kind, I was thinking. He is a dependable, decent man. There was goodness in him, yes, there was something of God in him. He is just a local man I employ to clean and see to the house, that's one way of looking at it. But. Something about Tom Quaye's care and loyalty, even if words like care and loyalty might usually suggest servility, is entrancing. He is like a big lump of medicine to me.

'Do you know, Tom, when this weather blows over, in a few weeks, you know, we might make that trip north.'

He turned his face to me, not on the same wavelength.

'What trip, major?' he said.

'We might make a run up on the Indian to see, you know, that wife of yours, and the two children.'

This was a possibility that had obviously never occurred to him. Perhaps he didn't even like the sound of it.

'To Titikope, major?'

'Yes, or you could just take the motorcycle, if you preferred.'

'No, I – I think this is one good idea.'

'Well, we can wait till the rains are done, and then make a plan. By the time these rains have finished we'll be stir-crazy, I'll be bound. We'll need a jaunt of some description. Unless you wanted to go alone as I say.'

'No, no, not alone, major,' said Tom.

'We can share the driving,' I said.

Tom looked at me as closely as I had looked at him.

His green eyes just stared at me. I was beginning to twitch with embarrassment. Then slowly, like the very rumble of the distant thunder outside, he started to laugh. He pointed his right hand at me, wagging it, making absolutely sure I got the joke. I got the joke. I laughed and laughed with him, under the enormous rain.

Chapter Twelve

Soon enough I was home. I had missed the birth by a few weeks. I came in the door and found Mai waiting for me in the narrow hall, one hand supporting herself against the wine-coloured wall. Her body was bent a little sideways, and I had to draw her into my arms to get a proper hold of her. I was concerned that the birth had weakened her so. But I could sense her enormous relief. She cried, and patted my chest. Such a moment of love that seemed. Then she brought me into the parlour to see Maggie. There is no experience in the world to match seeing your first child, for the first time. She was a little lost face in a nest of tiny blankets.

Mai on her own return had cut quite the figure in Sligo, my mother said, walking along Wine Street or O'Connell Street, crossing Grattan Bridge with her firm stride, going in and out of the fancier shops, drinking tea in the Café Cairo with all its hissing boilers and small-voiced maids, the fashionable ladies of Sligo arranged among the tables like the fabulous beasts of some impossible watering hole – in her Gibraltar coat, and the monkey swaying minutely on her shoulder. There was nothing else but Mai now in the talk of my mother. She thought her a rare person.

Yes, Mam cherished her. I wonder now if she didn't also invest Mai with some residual idea of her own real mother, whom she would never speak about. The spectre of illegitimacy kept her silent in her torment. But perhaps in Mam's mind her mother had been just such as Mai, tall, a touch theatrical, in well-chosen furs and dresses. Certainly, when I saw them together on the street, you couldn't help seeing, as I said, due to their very different heights, a mother and child.

But my mother, not being in any way a stupid woman, also picked up other signals from Mai. For twenty years and more she had stitched pinafores and smocks for the women in the asylum, and she knew something of female distress. She had found Mai a number of times in the back bedroom, sunken in what Mam called 'black thoughts'.

Dr Snow had prescribed some pills – little white ones they were, like the buttons you might sew on a robin's waistcoat.

When April came around we were not able to honour Maria Sheridan's call to go to Omard for the mayfly. But Mai said we would go next year for certain. She didn't feel quite up to it with the baby, and what she called 'a bit of lethargy' that she was feeling.

A few months later, I was sitting beside her in the tiny parlour in John Street. Our baby was sleeping in her Moses basket, there were no lamps or candles lit, and only the murmuring glow of the fire, now in its last hour of burning, played across Mai's features. Outside, Sligo town was silent in the deep, camphory folds of darkness and rain, the small hours given over only to last wanderers home, and Old Keighron's horse clopping past to the bakery. Mai was as still as a cat. It was so quiet we could hear Maggie breathing, a sound all smallness and quaintness that would make a darkened criminal smile in recognition. My father was off with his band somewhere, and my mother had kindly taken herself off to a Redemptorist mission with her own mother, or I should say her foster mother, Ma Donnellan. There was a fiery young curate in town now, a Father Gaunt, that Mam thought was Jesus returned to the earth.

The monkey sat by the fender, as contemplative as ourselves, and Mam's cat beside him, licking her thin arms. There was a dark, introspective unsmilingness to Mai's face, and yet in that moment I sensed that she was happy.

I was thinking of the poem by Coleridge, where he describes himself seated by just such a fire, his own child asleep in her cot beside him, and the film of ash on the grate, trembling in some tiny wind, putting him in mind of his own state, private, alone, in some lost evening of 1798. The eyes of the cat took the small firelight into their green depths. The monkey snaked out a skinny arm, and with great delicacy, plucked out one of the cat's eyes. Mai leaped to her feet, consternated, wrenched from her daydream.

When my mother returned, disclosure had to be made. Mai made her a pot of tea, and put her to bed.

The next day she telephoned to Dublin Zoo and they said they would be glad to have a Diana monkey. Mai left me to look after things, and went up to Dublin on the train, and deposited the creature among his own kind in the monkey house.

'A one-eyed cat is better than no cat,' said my mother, philosophically.

Dr Snow was a regular visitor, trying to help Mai with the breast milk, which was awfully hard for her, my mother said. She couldn't keep a proper supply going. A wet nurse was engaged from Far Finisklin but sent home again by Mam as she said the girl was not washed.

Mai wanted to see her brother Jack. He turned up in a new Crossley coupé, that gleamed even in the metal Sligo air. I was walking up John Street after a quick visit to the bookies when I saw him alight from the tremendous car, as neat and dark as a bishop.

'Ho, Jack Kirwan!' I called to him.

I let him in the little front door. Jack nodded at Mam as if he wasn't quite sure who she was, but then, that was always his manner, vague, and confusing to the mortals he laboured to engage with. Then it was up the coffin-narrow stairs to the back bedroom, which, when Jack stepped into it, suddenly looked like one of those old illustrations in *Alice in Wonderland*. It was clear enough from the gaze he gave me that he wanted to speak to Mai alone. The sun had come out in Mai's heart, that was for sure, to judge by her smile of welcome.

I stayed in the scullery helping Mam to cut the mutton for the evening meal. Maggie woke and my mother fed her from the curiously shaped bottle. Bound in swaddling clothes, nevertheless her feet, in violet pampooties – the epitome of infant style, since Mai had had them specially made by Johnston's of O'Connell Street, from an illustration in a Paris magazine – wriggled and turned.

Then Jack came down, followed by Mai.

'Jack, Jack,' said Mai, 'he is giving us Grattan House. What do you make of that?'

I was gobsmacked. Giving us Grattan House!

'That is extraordinarily generous,' I said to him, 'but we couldn't hope to recompense you properly for that.' I was dizzy now. Did he expect money from us? Was he selling at a 'friendly' price?

'He's *giving* it to us,' said Mai. 'Oh, Jack,' she said, meaning her brother, not myself, 'I don't think I can

ever be unhappy again, not if I can hang my hat in Grattan House!'

'Well, well,' said Jack. 'You'll be doing me a favour,
Mai. Get it off my hands. Sitting empty. A house needs
people in it. I am settled in Roscommon. Who better
than my own sister?'

This was an enormous speech for Jack. Even Mai
looked at him as if he were Edmund Burke of a sudden,
teasing out a thought in the House of Commons.

❧

Watching Tom through the open door as I am writing
this, I can just make out what he is doing, as he sways
about, chopping, gathering. It is so violently hot he is
wearing what amounts to a garment of sweat. The rains
cascade mercilessly outside. The roof has a hundred lunatic drummers beating on it. It is a belligerent cacoph-
ony, chaotic, but weirdly peaceful.

Tom Quaye's 'Capital' Braised Beef: Melt an ounce
of dripping in your stewing pot, brown 1 lb. of chopped
beef. Remove beef. Fry carrots, turnips and onions, add
half pint stock. Return meat, cover pot, simmer for an
hour. Bob's your uncle.

'That's capital,' I said, the first time he served it.

'Do you want the "Capital", major?' he might say
now, when he has found decent beef in the market.

I usually mash it up into a hash. Just the job.

If you wonder why
Old soldiers never die,
Fall in, fall in,
And follow your uncle Bob.

❧

Mai never spoke now of going to Dublin and making a name for herself in government circles and she took to speaking of the new people who had just been elected with humorous disparagement. But then, it was the era of disappointment and disillusionment. A great effort of the spirit had been expended in creating a new country. Inevitably it couldn't match expectations. Especially when De Valera came to power in '32, the so-called loser of the civil war.

'Pappy was right,' Mai said, 'we should have stuck with old John Redmond, for these lads are not the lads we thought they were.'

But she didn't follow my brother Tom, in her mind or otherwise, towards the likes of General O'Duffy, she didn't like the cut of him. One of Mai's friends in Galway was Rosie Fine, the daughter of Fine the pawnbroker. When Tom made casual remarks about Jews, aping O'Duffy, Mai would tense up with exasperation.

'This is just stupidity,' she would say, and shake her head. When Tom reminded Mai that O'Duffy had been Collins's right-hand man while he lived, Mai snorted.

'Collins would have horsewhipped him now,' she said.

It was exciting somehow to hear her talk in the old way. It strikes me now, if everyone had said, 'This is just stupidity,' we would never have had the war that eventually came.

Myself, I was finding it impossible to find good work as an engineer, and so went into the Land Commission as an assistant inspector. My career in the British Foreign Service didn't count for anything at home, and I was obliged to start off again. I purchased a nice little Baby Austin, because the work brought me all over Donegal, Leitrim and Cavan, carving up old places into serviceable farms and the like. But the pay was poor and I was struggling. Mai's joy in getting Grattan House endured, but it was an expensive property to run. When we went in first, the only things not mouldering in the salt air were the armies of dinner plates, carvers and saucers that Mai's mother had acquired over the decades, as well-to-do family members fell off their perches and left things in bequests. But the old curtains and carpets had to be replaced, and the legions of woodworm, rats, and mice gradually shown the door.

But Mai paid no blessed heed to this, parked her bag of gold sovereigns that had come to her from her mother, a remnant of an old legacy, in the cupboard with her mosquito boots and other retired gear from Africa. She gathered her acquaintance around her, and two or three nights a month cooked for her friends, or went off with Maggie to eat at their houses. Queenie Moran when she was up from Sligo, Rosie Fine – a little bevy of strong women that she had gathered to herself with some expertise in the line of friendship. I would often come home from a long run somewhere and, standing in the porch, hear inside the laughter of the women, and envy them somewhat. Men have less talent for such friendships maybe. She was in possession of the house she loved, in the city that she approved of. Galway was held higher in her heart than Dublin, though she liked very much to go on excursions there, to shop in Switzer's for the latest clothes, and Weir's for bracelets and rings, and to go to the theatre or the concert, always taking the same room in her favoured hotel in Kildare Street. And speaking of approval, how many dresses and coats and blouses came down to her from the great department stores in Dublin 'on approval'. You couldn't count them.

A year after Maggie, Ursula was born. Two children in the space of two years, which was hard for Mai, and apart from anything else, costly for a junior man in the Land Commission.

Nevertheless, Mai in full stride along the esplanade at Salthill was a sight, the little Kerry maid pushing the perambulator, the two dogs skittering and scattering about. She loved the sea wind, the rougher the better. Maggie's hand in her mother's, with her black hair blowing in the wind and her Parisian coat. As soon as Mai got the signal from her magazines to wear trousers, she donned them, jodhpurs at first, and then loose pyjama-like affairs that seemed to help her sail along. She had a 'Jersey' swimsuit and didn't scorn to enter the cold waters in it, breasting the waves and swimming far out into the bay. This caused, both the trousers and the swimming out so far, equal scandal in Salthill village. It was a rule with Mai when she encountered a child begging in the street, to press a sixpence into the outstretched paw. The righteous shook their heads.

Her other joy was murdering friends on the courts of the tennis club. After these games I would be given a full account, stroke by stroke, victory by victory, in the doss at night, the two of us ensconced in her father's regal old bed, she shadowing the games with demonstrations of a forward or backward drive, her long arms swishing about over the old damask covers and eiderdowns.

In the winter in that room it was so cold that a rheum of ice formed on everything, so that we awoke like arctic explorers after a light snow has fallen on them, and it took a prayer and a curse to get us out of bed and into our clothes.

The other great joy of those days, separate and even secret from Mai, was the horse-racing. On my travels for the Land Commission I would often make a run sideways to a racecourse, little point-to-points on windy Donegal strands, or big meetings further afield, or failing that I would place my bets in any of the bookies' shops in Galway that were discreet and off the main streets.

Oh, Sligo racecourse, in the wild rains of spring, the intoxication of it. Or in the long evenings of summer, the most poetic racecourse in Ireland, Phoenix Park, worth the long drive back to Galway in the small hours, passing through the little sleeping towns and villages, buoyed up occasionally by an unexpected win, the wipers flashing back and forth like an afflicted metronome. Perhaps there were more losses than wins, in the upshot. Many, many losses. My great failing it is true was spending whole nights studying the form sheets and then, in a form of admirable cowardice, backing the bloody favourites. But, but, Phoenix Park, with the great trees around the enclosure, and the air of conspiracy every last thing possessed, the smart wooden buildings, the carved clocks, the eccentric old tipsters who never left the bar to watch a race, the bookies up on their boxes, crying out their information in strange codes, the trainers' secrets spreading out from stable boys and infecting every conversation with anxiety and excitement, the summer wind moving through the trees, and the crowds roaring, roaring like the very choir of life. All those matters gladdened me, and no distance would have been too great to go.

By this time my brother Tom had been going out with Roseanne Clear for years.

Roseanne's father had been in the old police force, just like brother Eneas, and had got himself into a whole lot of bother during the civil war, and was said to have been murdered in cold blood by the new National Army. After independence of course that would have been, so her father would have been no longer an RIC man by then, because they had been disbanded. But it was said he had tried to ingratiate himself with the new crowd by informing in some fashion or another – and informing was certainly in fashion just then. He went the way of all informers in Ireland and was killed. None of this deterred Tom. But now we were back from Africa, Mai made it her business to take him aside and explain a few things to him, that going out and an engagement were two different things, and marriage another thing again. Tom took it all in good part, and anyway, he wasn't in disagreement, no, he was well smitten.

The Mam was none too keen on her, not only because she was a Presbyterian, but because she said every blessed man in Sligo looked at her 'in the wrong way', and she didn't think a woman should be playing the piano in a dance band.

But despite that, Tom married her. They had to go to Dublin to get the job done discreetly. Mai was her bridesmaid. That must have been 1934, a couple of years after De Valera got into power, and knocked Tom's political ambitions out of kilter. He was running with that O'Duffy character, as near to a little Irish Mussolini as you could get, but there was no talking to him about it, and somehow or other marrying Roseanne Clear got bound into all that, like a corncrake is sometimes bound into a sheaf of corn by the careless reaper.

That was the news then, that was how things went on.

Chapter Thirteen

Then there came one afternoon two gentlemen from the bank. The manager himself, Mr Tuohy, and his assistant.

It was a blustery day in summer, the wind stirring in the east.

Mr Tuohy had an impressive goitre under his chin, which had altered his speech, so that he seemed to sing rather than talk, in a melancholy plainchant. He was a man of a generally exhausted demeanour, who was said to be a demon for the seaweed baths in Enniscrone. He was thin, so that in the distance, in his black suit, he always looked like a pencil mark.

Mai knew Mr Tuohy better than myself, though he had facilitated a few loans for me in recent times. The house of course was held in my name and was good collateral, and small loans had been issued to me with a smile.

The Kerry maid brought them into the sitting room, where Mai was licking through the pages of *La Femme chic* (always an embarrassing item to pick up at the paper shop, where it came on special order – 'Mr McNulty, your French magazine . . .'), and I was reading through the racing paper, readying for another descent on some distant racecourse. Mai rose, and looked pleased to see them, if surprised. She told the maid to fetch some tea but Mr Tuohy it seemed was not thirsty and he didn't consult his abashed-looking assistant. So we all sat down again, and smiled at each other.

Mr Tuohy gazed out for a few moments at the white horses moving across the bay, nodded his head, making his swollen underchin wobble.

'Such a fine property,' he said. 'I have noted from the deeds that your father purchased it all of sixty years ago, Mrs McNulty. That is a long time to have something in the family. And so nice to come in and hear the voices of the little ones. I know it will be exceptionally hard for you.'

This caught Mai off guard, if not quite myself.

'Exceptionally hard?' she said.

There had been a few letters regarding the loans, more than a few, which I had assiduously read. Deep in my heart I knew why he had come. But I was alarmed, sickened. I held onto the arms of my chair and uttered without speaking, privately in my burning brain, a hasty and heartfelt prayer. How successfully, in the great effort to keep everything shipshape and afloat and going forward, I had blanked out the possibility of this terrible event. It was a talent, I was desperately thinking, a talent, and now in payment for this talent would come the inquisition.

'Excuse me, Mr Tuohy, but I have no idea what you are talking about,' said Mai, in her pleasant Galway accent, even and musical in its own way.

'I have written extensively to Mr McNulty, kept him fully abreast of things. He knew when he took the loans that they needed repaying, and that when you give something as collateral, of course that is the item that must eventually be surrendered in order to honour the repayment of the loans, if not otherwise attended to.'

I could tell from Mr Tuohy's tone that he had opted to spell everything out as if we were children. Mai was no child. She was looking at Mr Tuohy now as if she had enlarged to ten times her size. I thought the four walls might be sundered by her gaze and washed out into the wind-ruined sea. To say I felt embarrassed now could not begin to describe the feeling. I sat there, cancelled out, even to myself, and then came the moment when Mai turned her face to me, that striking, smooth-featured, bright-eyed, now smouldering face.

'Jack?' she said, and only that.

'Well,' I said, in a triumph of feebleness, 'there have been a few loans, that's true.'

'Mr McNulty,' said Mr Tuohy, 'I have no wish to contradict you in your own sitting room, but the whole purpose of my visit today is to explain the necessity for selling the house immediately. You are many hundreds of pounds in debt.'

'Jack,' she said again, this time much quieter.

Guilt, dreadful guilt, was now stealing upon me.

'There has been absolutely,' began Mr Tuohy, and here his assailed voice cracked a moment, so he attempted the word again, 'absolutely no attempt, *no* attempt, made to repay, so our interest in the property is now to the entire value of same. It is my solemn and bounden duty to dispose of it. I am so sorry, Mrs McNulty.'

Then his assistant spoke for the first and last time:

'Indeed,' he said, as if the obvious pain in Mai's face forbade him to maintain his silence, even if his employer had impressed on him the need to keep silent at all times in such a delicate situation.

Mai said 'Hmm,' and flounced her head, and stared out into the bay. 'Hmm,' she said again. I thought for one helpful moment that she had forgiven me, or that indeed this event fulfilled a desire she had hidden from me, to be rid of the house maybe . . .

'But,' she said. 'There is no problem with money. If it's just money you need . . .' And she moved towards the door. 'I have funds, Mr Tuohy, that you won't be aware of. You see, we don't keep everything in the bank. Oh, no,' she said, laughing now. 'Just you wait here a moment, and I will show you.'

'Where are you going, Mai?' I said, now doubly, trebly, alarmed.

'You'll see, Mr Tuohy,' she said, and went out on her errand. We sat on, Mr Tuohy nodding now and again as if in further conversation with himself, and offering me a half-extinguished smile, and I heard Mai's step on the stairs, going up in a hurry to our bedroom. I heard her high heels – two-tone leather – stamp across the Persian carpet and the polished boards to the cupboard, I could picture it in my head, perfectly, and heard the door open, and heard more dimly her scrambling about in the ordered debris of our time in Africa, looking confidently, I supposed, for the bag of coins. Then I heard, if you can hear such a thing, the gap of silence, of disbelief, of her brain whirring, trying to reach a good thought, a good explanation, had Jack put them in the bank after all? Had she in a vague moment? Why, she hadn't looked in that little bag for five years, had she? Or had she moved them somewhere else in the house, where were they, where were they?

No good answers coming to her, and no sign of her fortune, she was obliged to retrace her steps, across the handsome carpet, and down the well-trimmed stairs, and across the gaping sorrow of the hallway, and back to us in the sombre room, and she could do no other than to return with her heart half broken, but ready in a crazy instant to be reassured, restored, and then she stood there, looking out at the now thunderous waves, muted behind the old window glass, as she had done before, the gap of aeons between the two actions. And I knew she wanted to speak, but it was as if she hadn't the energy to form one word. And not having really the desire to do so, in case in the upshot of her speaking there would be an answer. Fully for five minutes she maintained her silence, like a diver balanced out on the lip of the board, ready to spring out, leap out, through the clear air, and then, because there was nothing else to be done, she turned her face away from the sea, and with a withering strength, a strength despite everything, looked again at me, and smiled, smiled gorgeously, that smile that was part of the reason I loved her and had pursued and married her, a smile I set such store on I couldn't help but smile back at now. Mai, standing there – even now, sitting in Africa, writing this, I mourn that moment, even as I feel the terror of it.

'All the money, Jack, all the money,' she said. There was still love in her voice, as August still has the summer in it. But also the desolation of winter.

Grattan House was sold. Now all the truth was out, and like most truth that is eventually revealed after long hiding, it was little or no use to Mai, certainly not to me. Yes, I had made dozens of little visits to the cupboard, for racing debts, for debts at the dress shops and the hat shops, for bills that came down from Switzer's and Weir's, for this, for that, and for the other thing. Each time reaching into the bag without disturbing it too much, not wanting to know too much about what I was doing, thinking each time, 'It's just a few coins, there are plenty there yet,' until the vile day when my hand went in and even a man making the greatest effort in the history of the world not to notice something, noticed that what I fetched out was the last sovereign.

❧

The guilt attached to 'losing' Grattan House is still profound, eternal, and terrifying. But at the time I am not sure I fully understood what I had done.

Looking back now, sitting in this simple clay and wooden room in Accra, it is clear that it was a time to lay my heart bare to her, to talk to her about how we lived, and to beg her to forgive me for what had happened. But I did none of those things.

❧

I settled her bills at Divilly's butchers and Mrs Synott's grocery shop in Salthill, and my bar bill at the Bal, utilising my very last resources, just not quite able to leave them in the lurch, the house was put on the market and sold in a thrice to a friend of Mr Tuohy's, and off we went, lock, stock and barrel, or lockless, stockless and barrel-less, to a 'nice little house' in Magheraboy in Sligo, which Pappy was able to get a hold of from one of his butties, for a sum so tiny that Mai, mysteriously enough, slapped her two hands on her thighs when I told her, whether out of disgust at our new status, or delight at the affordability of Sligo, I couldn't quite tell – but probably not the latter.

Because, as if it were a sort of hidden illness in McNulty marriages, she had stopped talking to me directly, as Mam had done with Pappy. If we had had tea at my Mam's house now, it would surely have been a complicated evening. As Mai had no liaison officer of the age of reason in the house, but only two streeling children, this scheme of indirect speech was very tricky for her fully to effect, and occasionally she was obliged by blind necessity to say something, in which case she kept it short, clipped, and to the point, like the orders of a superior officer.

And she insisted on separate bedrooms.

Although it caused me immense pain, I also thought there was some justice in her stance, and prayed nightly on the narrow couch which was now my bed that there might be some truth in the saying that time will heal all wounds. But her despair, her air of hopelessness and outrage, was frightening to behold, and I was drinking as fast and as much as I could in the evenings in the cold, dank bars of Sligo town to try and erase the floating image in my brain of the tall, thin, white-faced ghost that was now my wife. One night I headed home so drunk that I was looking everywhere for Grattan House, in the muddled misconception it was still our home, searching up and down the streets of Sligo for a house that was in another city.

I was not entirely hopeless though. She was still nearby, and I had a belief that whatever bound us would eventually be restored. I said as much to Tom and he nodded in sage silence.

I would have to hole up like Jesse James in my own house, and hope fervently for a pardon, if not from Mai, then from the Secret Judge of life. And pray that we might find a firm footing again in the ordinary carnival of things.

Chapter Fourteen

It was a mean little house, it was true. But it had room for the two babies and even the strange dislocations of their parents, and it bore a better relation to my actual income. Out back was a lonesome square of grass and dandelions, and the wind twisted itself into the desolate space and ran its chilly fingers through the grass, and asked the time from the dandelion heads. The houses were new, built as a little speculation by a builder from Rossaveal, far enough away in Connemara to be unavailable when a slate began its slide down the roof, or his sewerage pipes parted underground.

In the first summer was the small mercy that Mai discovered Gibraltar, a concrete sea-baths that had been built on the stony lip of the shore in Far Finisklin. There was a big lump of a rock abutting it, hence the name, and here Mai spread herself on hot days, and made a little kingdom of her towel, her bag, and her clothes, and had Maggie for a border guard at her feet. Ursula was deposited at their grandparents', my Mam toiling to bring the great pram over the inconvenient granite step of her front door. Indeed Mai had pleased Mam by naming Ursula after St Ursula of the Ursulines. My mother was a great liker of religious orders and indeed had promised my sister Teasy many years before to the Sisters of Nazareth House, and had delivered her to their premises in Bexhill-on-Sea when she was fourteen, where now she thrives as a mendicant nun among the little hills and backways of East Sussex.

Mam had a special love for Ursula, initially through the very act of naming her. Mai had greeted her suggestion that Ursula be also promised to the nuns without enthusiasm, though Mai in her own way was just as religious as Mam.

'I think one McNulty is enough for any order to cope with,' Mai said.

My mother laughed heartily.

'You may be right, Mai, you may be right.'

Maggie was in Low Babies at school now and full of talk, and her first job as a talker was official intermediary between her mother and me.

There was the rash of 'jiltses and shams' from the town that also spread themselves on Gibraltar, and raised cries and tidal waves by leaping into the sea from the rocky ledges. One summer evening, while she cooked in the back scullery, home from a long summer day of sunbathing and swimming – I could see the salt crystals drying on her face – I asked her whether she minded that she shared her Newfoundland with the savages.

'Tell your father I prefer their company to his,' she said to Maggie.

'Mammy says . . .' said Maggie.

'It's alright, Maggie,' I said. 'I got the message.'

One day later that same year, I got a card in an envelope from her friend Queenie Moran, to ask if she might meet with me privately in the town. This was an unusual communication, in that I had never had much dealings with Queenie, except in so far as she was Mai's friend. Queenie sometimes sailed in for tea in Magheraboy. Then Maggie was put into her Shirley Temple dress and her black hair tortured into curls, and Mai would put her up on the sitting-room table to sing, as a hundred other little girls of Sligo were obliged to do in that era. And a very good fist Maggie made of it, tap-dancing, curtsying, and singing out the songs.

So I stared a while at Queenie's card, looking at the handsome swirls of her handwriting. But the words were polite, and I couldn't see the harm in it, and I agreed to meet her in Lyons' cafe, a premises that Mai herself did not frequent.

It was a Saturday morning and I went forth in my best bib and tucker, although I had a murderous headache from the night before. I had shaved and swallowed a raw egg with a little brandy to make some amends to my innards. There was a danger from a Saturday morning, in that Mai did like to make her pilgrimage among the shops with Maggie, something Maggie herself delighted in. It gave me heart to think Mai had devised a method and routine for living in Sligo, the town of her exile from Galway. Sligo did have a few beads on its thread, some good haberdasheries and the like, not to mention in the evenings the otherworlds and swooning dreams of the Gaiety picture house. Mai still went to the pictures the way other mortals go to public houses, to be immersed in what to her was the opium of high fashion, trailing gowns, shimmering light, and Fred Astaire or suchlike singing his romantic songs, putting on a top hat, shooting a cuff, and shaking out a leg. So I was keeping a weather eye out to make sure she was not abroad on her travels, at least anywhere near Wine Street.

Here was Queenie now, who had chosen a more or less conspiratorial table out of the way of the various wives of Sligo having their Saturday treat. The place hummed with them, reminding me of the noise that starlings make. She stood when I approached the table and held out her hand for me to shake, removing the glove expertly as she did so. I felt her cold hand in mine, and was thinking idly what bad circulation she must have, for a district nurse indeed, to be cold in this overheated, muggy room, the Russian cigarettes in holders and the rough Sweet Afton fags mingling democratically in the air.

'Jack,' she said. 'It's really kind of you to see me. Truly.'

'Ah well, sure, Queenie, why not? It's not often I get a card from a lady, let me tell you, to be meeting her quietly somewhere.'

I got a little sense that she considered this remark off-colour, because her face showed the tiniest flinch, but whatever about that, she sat down, I sat down, after dragging off my greatcoat and throwing it across another chair, causing a little ruckus of anxiety to the women at the nearest table, as if the coat were a dead body.

'Will you have something, Jack?' she said, raising her left hand, ringless and white.

'No, no,' I said, 'no, not feeling the best, you know.'

She let the hand drift up further to her head and smoothed her red hair. Queer enough that Mai's best friend was a red-haired woman, and that I had red hair, and Ursula. If Ursula had been there we would have looked like a little family.

'Look, Jack,' she said, 'if there's one thing my father said to me, a thousand times, it was never to interfere in a marriage, never to come between a couple in any way, and, you know, Jack, he is a solicitor, and grapples with human matters every day. And I would not like you to think I was attempting to do that!'

She had spoken these words with some emphasis, as if she meant them maybe to be humorous, but mostly they alarmed me.

'The fact is, Jack, I am very worried about Mai.'

'Oh?'

'Are you sure you wouldn't like a cup of tea? You do seem a little peaky, Jack.'

'No, no, I'm fine, Queenie, fine . . . What is it then about Mai that troubles you?'

'Do you know,' she said, 'troubles me is the right phrase. I am troubled, I am. There are things she has said to me over the last year . . . I know you have had your difficulties . . . Although I don't know the details of course, and haven't asked her. But. Jack, do you know that when she was found to be pregnant with Ursula, she came to see me, in great floods of tears. She had come down on the bus from Galway, weeping. She said she just couldn't have another baby. She said – well, some terrible things . . .'

'What terrible things?' I said, thinking I might as well hear everything, I couldn't feel any more alarmed.

'She isn't – do you think . . . No, what am I saying . . . Technically, do you know, as a nurse, Jack, and I am not a doctor, but do you know, there is a sadness in her sometimes, am I shocking you when I say that?'

'What do you mean?' I said, admittedly getting a touch angry suddenly. Just a touch. What was she suggesting, that Mai was unwell in some way? As a child of the Sligo asylum I was not going to have this woman tell me my wife was . . .

'What are you trying to say?' I said, undoubtedly somewhat stonily.

'Is there any chance you think that maybe Mai suffers from her nerves?'

'Well,' I said, 'no, I don't believe so, Queenie, and I must say I'm with your father there on his very wise advice not to interfere in people's lives, I must say, I really must, Queenie now.'

'I'm not putting it right. I am making a terrible mess of this. Please, Jack, forgive me. All this weighs so on my mind, and she says things to me, and I wonder is she saying the same things to you, or to anyone, maybe lovely Maria Sheridan, or her brother, such a lovely man too . . .'

Then she was silent. She had reached the place we all reach when we are trying to help someone, but find there is a great ditch between our help and the object of our help. A yawning and unhelpful gap. I felt suddenly sorry for her. Queenie Moran, spinster, district nurse, daughter of a Galway solicitor, trying to broach a horrible subject with the husband of her dear friend.

'Look it, Queenie,' I said, 'I appreciate you writing to me. Something is on your mind. Rest assured that Mai is fine. My God, ain't she always feisty? Yes, she is. She talks wild talk sometimes. She brings her thoughts to extremes certainly. But look, Queenie, she's Mai McNulty, Mai Kirwan as was, did you ever meet in your life a more . . .'

But I couldn't think of the phrase I needed to describe her. I realised I had become emotional now, there was a miniature rivulet of a tear coming down my cheek, which she might interpret hopefully as the result of my hangover.

'It's just, Jack,' she said, in a little resigned tone, as if she had decided now to breach her father's advice after all, 'if I say nothing, and something awful happens, I would never, ever forgive myself.'

Now I was silent, looking at her. Maybe I twitched an eyebrow, because she responded as if I had encouraged her, though I would have been glad as a rose if she had just disappeared now in a puff of smoke, like the unwelcome genie she seemed to me in that moment.

'Do you know, when Ursula was born, she said to me she wished she could kill the child, kill it, that's what she said, she sat there in the Café Cairo, just a couple of years ago, hissing with anger and God knows what, and said she wanted to kill the baby because it had red hair. That's not sensible, Jack. I reminded her I had red hair. She sat there in the Café Cairo and told me she had no maternal instinct whatsoever, which was hard for me to hear because, because . . . Because I do love that girl, Jack, everybody loves her that knows her . . . Such things to be saying. And even before Ursula was born, for heaven's sake, Jack, she said that she would deal with the matter next chance she got, she would drink a bottle of gin in a hot bath, she begged me to tell her how to get rid of the baby, Jack, don't you see, the horror of a conversation like that, with your own childhood friend?'

Now Queenie was weeping openly, and it is impossible to be angry with a weeping person, I have found.

'But, Queenie, she did none of those things.'

'But she tried, Jack, she tried, I know she did, she drank the bottle of gin, she sat in a hot bath, she did everything she could, I know she did, and I should have told you before, now I see I should, because of the other thing she said, when Ursula was born, and her without a shred, without a shred she said, of feeling for either of them . . .'

'No, no,' I said, but wondering had she taken the chance to try to do something grievous when I was away on Land Commission business, 'we were still in Grattan House when Ursula was born, we were still – ' I was going to say, in the same bedroom, but of course I did not, 'and anyway, she's very fond of Maggie, and very much devoted to Ursula, oh, yes,' I said, 'she is a splendid mother, don't pay any heed to her.'

'But, Jack,' she said.

What? I thought. There was a longer silence then.

The women at the nearest table were queerly quiet, so that I feared they were listening to all this. Maybe they knew me, maybe they knew Mai. Oh, Queenie, Queenie, I thought, take your lousy truth away with you. If you take it away I won't have to think about it, I will banish it from my mind.

'She told me, Jack, she has made, you know . . .'

'What?' I said, in the greatest despair. I knew she would tell all now, and I didn't want her, God forgive me, to tell all. Better the fog than the clearing weather.

'Attempts,' said Queenie, as if hoping the one word would suffice, and she wouldn't have to say any more.

'Attempts?' I said, shivering suddenly in the fuggy room, glancing at the other table, throwing a little brief smile their way. Whatever you can hear of this, pay no heed, pay no heed.

'Yes. Dr Snow, you know.'

'What, Dr Snow?'

'Prescribed her these pills, you know, and she said, she said she took a lot of them one night, this was just a month ago, washed down with gin . . .'

'Look, Queenie,' I said, laughing then, laughing. 'Mai doesn't even drink. She has never touched a drop of alcohol in her whole life. Never.'

Queenie looked at me, not knowing in the least what to say to me. I suddenly felt mortally foolish, ignorant, small. Of course, Mai could have been smoking opium for all I knew, and dancing naked about her bedroom, because after nine at night I didn't see her again till morning. That's how it was in those days, and I lived in hopes of a better time. I lived in hope of a reconciliation, the way real couples do, the way ordinary decent people do, eventually, in the upshot, after time has healed all wounds.

'She has never touched a drop in all her days,' I said again, as if this were a religious tenet.

'Oh, Jack, oh, Jack,' she said, weeping.

The air went out of me.

Chapter Fifteen

When I got back to Magheraboy I found she was out with Maggie after all though I had not seen them in the town. I went up to her room to look around. I didn't feel I should be in there, poking about, but if I was longing to find something it was evidence that what Mai had said to Queenie was fanciful nonsense, or that Queenie had gone mad.

The room, as I expected it would be, was beautifully arranged. The old marriage bed was carefully made, Bristol fashion. On the sugar-twist side table her fashion magazines were in a neat stack, her reading glasses waiting on top. The grate was swept clean and a scuttle of coal all ready. Two mezzotints, of her father and her mother in their heyday, were framed each side of the fireplace, her father looking quite cross but magisterial. The carpet-sweeper had recently done its work. The curtains she had saved from Grattan House and adapted for this humbler window, old scenes of rural France in red and white, were almost closed, discreetly and demurely.

I began to feel very sad. Not because I thought her room was sad, but because it reminded me how happily in the main we had lived together. It was a room without me in it, though I stood in it now. I looked in the wardrobe and there were only her clothes hanging there, whereas once it had held my suits and waistcoats too. I didn't now for a moment believe Queenie. I would have seen signs of it, signs of such great distress – I would have known at the time, of course I would have. She never showed the children anything but love. Maybe she was a bit fonder of Maggie, but still Ursula was looked after carefully – spoiled really, the two of them.

In the drawer of her dressing table right enough were a few bottles of those little tablets. Only one of them had pills in it, and the date on it was recent. Was that a good or a bad thing? I had thought, right enough, that the pills had been only to get her through a bumpy time, when she was pregnant with Maggie. Still and all, these were private matters – women's trouble, as my Mam would have put it. I had no right to be rummaging there, and concocting theories.

In the bottom drawer were her silk knickers for special occasions and her better brassieres, and her copy of *Married Love*, that many a Sligo woman at that time had in her knicker drawer. Wrapped in one of her mother's best tea-towels was the red-tinted Venetian tumbler her father had used for his one glass of whisky on a Saturday. Tucked in neatly, like bits of ordnance, were two bottles

of gin, one three-quarters empty, one full. Would these
date from the time Queenie said she had swallowed pills,
or the time she was pregnant with Ursula – the hot bath
and the gin? – I couldn't believe they did. I didn't believe
either thing had really happened. I couldn't allow that
she wanted to kill poor Ursula, just because she had red
hair. Ridiculous! Maybe poor Queenie was drinking,
maybe poor Queenie was going mad. Hearing voices,
imagining things. Because this was Mai McNulty's bedroom, shipshape and composed, and even if there were
these little bits of evidence, I knew in my heart it was the
truth, the gospel truth, that Mai had never drunk a drop
of alcohol in her life. It was part of her legend. Even nuns
drank on the western seaboard of Ireland. But not Mai,
not Mai Kirwan, no, most certainly not. Mai who plainly
loved her children, and if she and I were going through
a rough patch, all would surely be mended at length.
Mai, Mai, whom I loved to distraction, Mai who was
too proud and good to drink bloody alcohol, she could
leave that to the rest of us! And what of it if she did want
to drink a few glasses in the evening, even alone in her
bedroom, she was perfectly entitled, there was no harm
in it as such, no, not at all, but it was a definite and palpable truth, that Mai McNulty, née Kirwan, had never,
had never touched a drop in her born days. And therefore could never, ever, have sought to take her life, or the

life of her unborn baby, it was not possible, not remotely possible, and anyone who said otherwise was a pitiful liar.

Mai came home, sprightly, with far fewer parcels than in the old days, just some little bargains she had picked up on her way, not paying much heed to me, plonking some vegetables into the scullery for washing later. Then she brought Maggie into the sitting room, and got her over by the good light at the window, because she wanted to run the nit comb through her head of thick hair. She stood there, in the painterly light, expertly drawing the comb through the strands, peering at the head for eggs, and seeming quite content in those moments, and oblivious, and not in any way fitting the description of a suicide or a murderer.

When Maggie had run out again into the haggard patch of garden to play, I geared myself up. My first obstacle was her practised ignoring of me, the first thing I prayed would go in the hoped-for healing. Because it was very painful, very diminishing as one might say.

'Mai,' I said, 'do you mind if I ask you a question?'

It occurred to me that it might be more efficacious if I could tie her down and question her under pain of torture, I might have a better chance of getting an answer. But I had to try. I was already feeling routed, before I had even begun, in the face of her lack of response. She was checking the comb in the windowlight for those rascally eggs.

'I don't want to talk, Jack.'

'I know, Mai, but we haven't really talked about anything for about – is it a year?'

'I don't really feel like talking, Jack.'

'Mai, can I just say, I am really really sorry for what I did, I am really sorry about everything, I mean, desolate to have caused you such grief, and I absolutely understand how you are feeling, and I believe you are quite entitled to feel monumentally angry, and you must go on feeling angry of course if that is how it must be. But I wonder if I have apologised properly. I thought of writing you a letter, but here we are in our own house, and I just wish to say it clearly, because things are not always said clearly in life, I have found. I am sorry, I am very sorry, and what's more I love you and revere you and just want you to be happy again.'

I saw her pause in her examination of the comb. I felt like Cicero might have when he had at last managed to get some argument written out in defence of a client. For the first time in many months, I felt relieved, lighter, more I suppose of a man. Not a gentleman, I knew, but a man for all that. She was looking at the comb, moving her closed lips back and forward across each other slowly.

'Are you, Jack?' she said then.

'I could have sorry carved into my forehead and it wouldn't tell you how sorry I am. I regret my stupidity, my bloody stupidity. I don't think you should forgive me, as a matter of fact, because I believe the whole matter was unforgivable.'

Now she nodded her head, not in order to agree or disagree, I thought, but simply as a reflection of her thinking mind. Everything held still for about a minute. Another minute. Another.

'I accept your apology,' she said.

'What?' I said.

She turned around, and looked me square in the face, across the ten feet that separated us. Across the hundred miles.

'I have been so lonely,' she said, just that, and hovered there, holding the comb still. I stepped forward and crossed the little Persian carpet, and got to her as quickly as I could without knocking her over. I thought she was going to faint. Her head had dropped and her eyes closed, and her whole body seemed to droop, as if she had been holding up the sky with her head, and someone had just put in a pillar for it instead. I had seen construction workers with just that reaction, trying to get in a bridge support. I put my arms around her, feeling such great relief that I think I cried out briefly, and she put her arms around me. We just stood there for fifteen minutes, maybe more, holding on, feeling slightly ridiculous and wondrously happy.

1938, three years later. It was as if the bricks and mortar of the house itself were saturated in alcohol. As if the house itself were drinking. There was something enjoyable about some of it, at least at the beginning, at least at the beginning of certain evenings. As it was my custom to bring friends and cronies home after the pubs closed, there might be a good crowd of people in the front room in the small hours. There would be singing, especially when Tom was there with a couple of his band members, you'd hear 'The Leitrim Lass', which was Tom's most requested tune, and sometimes the noise made was very pleasant, with Joe Burns as may be making the very plaster shift on the ceiling with his clarinet. And Mai's old piano in the corner would not be neglected, and there were plenty of hands that played. And I would look forward to singing 'Roses of Picardy'.

Eventually, after many evenings, many months and months of evenings, Mai appeared in the room at last, a tiny bit thrown sideways by whatever she had been drinking in truth, but properly dressed, and in a pleasant good humour, and she sat down at the piano and started to play 'Let's Keep the Party Clean', while I did the words in my best mock-English accent.

Don't give way to the old temptation
Of treating simple virtue with a sneer.

Then Pappy played a suite of reels and jigs, which led to clumsy dancing. But Tom was well known for his old-fashioned solo dancing, and he stood up now on Mr Kirwan's solid dining-room table, throwing caution to the wind, and clattered out his dance, his arms fastened to his sides in the best style, only his fingers slightly stirring, and everything a mighty blur from the knee down of swirling sideways moves of the shinbones, and banging shoes.

And in Mai there was suddenly a strange and wonderful gaiety, and something of the reason why all the friends of her youth loved her shone out. And there was a happiness in all that, even if it was the happiness of people lifted out of themselves by the drinking. But didn't the Romans themselves, who had the best of everything, say life would be intolerable without it? Certainly I believe my life would have been, even if the intolerability of life was caused in some part by the very cure for it. Because as the night wore on, there would always be a great if gradual sea change, not only in Mai, but in the company generally, like children obliged to pay the price eventually for their happiness. And then there were bleak faces as blanched as moons, and weary bodies stumbling forward into the darkness of Magheraboy, and words of farewell thrown back in muddled grunts and whispers.

And then as Mai went back up the stairs, I might see the faces of Maggie and Ursula looking down at us through the banisters, not quite young courtiers gazing down on the gay and bright life of adults, but witnesses maybe mostly of their darknesses. And always I remember in myself the confused desire to follow her, and the flooding hope that she might turn on the stair and beckon me, but no, that was a great rarity, and usually she would not – for our rapprochement reached but seldom to sharing a bed – and I would return to the now empty room, with its plates of cigarette stubs and cigars, the bottles fallen over like so many little towers, and take up my station on the couch. And curious to me now that in all that there was a sort of contentment, and even in the hard sickness of the morning a certain wry amusement at it all, as if a man may find comfort in the unexpected humour of his execution.

Chapter Sixteen

As an experiment in going out without actually bringing mayhem to Osu, and feeling mightily stir-crazy, I
drove off alone last night to sample the fare of the Regal cinema. When I say drove, I mean mostly skidded
and squelched about, but I made it. There were dozens
of couples in the nice good humour of people released
from daily lives, and though I was alone, and, as I saw
from my visage briefly in the window of the ticket kiosk,
had gone somewhat beetroot from the rain and heat on
my face, I didn't feel I was being unduly stared at. There
were no other white faces in the audience, and the film
was one of those mysterious epics made by the Gold
Coast Film Unit, and also an old picture from the late
thirties, it looked like, about cattlemen in Colorado. I
had a lovely time, eating out of a box of local chocolates
that tasted curiously of childhood.

✿

Around that time we were sent word that Nicholas
Sheridan had died and would we cross to Omard for the
funeral. Well, there was no doubt that we would, but it

presented a difficulty for Mai. In the first place, the grief of the news utterly dismayed her. I could see when I went up to her bedroom and told her, she in her long blue silken dressing gown that would not have disgraced a Hollywood star, if a little less clean than it should have been, with smears across the lap and breast where she had eaten her dinners alone over the months, that this was news she was no longer able to bear with equanimity, if she ever had been. She looked at me with her open stare and wailed out a long streeling cry, like some old mournful scene in a peasant play.

But now she would have to gird her loins in a fashion she had left behind her, maybe a year since, and clothe herself not only in her best black clothes, but also in the daily fortitude of ordinary persons, who understand what's what and what's required for the funeral of a beloved friend. I don't believe Mai thought she was up to the task, but nevertheless she bathed herself and got Maggie to run the brush through her hair the necessary hundred times, as in other days, as if about to venture out on a pilgrimage of the shops.

The children were put with their grandparents, and we headed east in the intrepid Austin, which by virtue of my work almost knew the way to Cavan on its own. How often I had run past Kilnaleck and decided not to venture in and see Nicholas and Maria, fearing their intelligence and the inability of my face to mask any

unpalatable truths. It seemed a long, long journey and
Mai said not a word the whole way, which is a fearsome
thing in a small motorcar. It was not that I felt hostility
from her. Now and then I would glance at her as she
peered forth it seemed without seeing through the rain-
speckled windscreen, and wondered at her state of mind.
She seemed folded into herself, folded flat, like some
linen to be stored away.

'Just pull over, Jack, for a minute,' she said, when we
got to the upper gates of Omard.

It was a place where she had been happy so many
times, as a girl and a young woman, and it seemed she
needed a few minutes to allow an echo of that happiness
to touch her. I knew she was trying to inflate herself,
organ by inner organ, find a semblance of her old character, the indomitable young woman who by sheer force
of character was so famously 'loved by all'. The woman
whose force in those early days oftentimes had left me
oddly abashed. This effort to refind herself now filled
me with worry and watchfulness.

The day had been unsettled and now and then a wind
buffeted the motorcar. Fifteen minutes passed, half an
hour. Still Mai sat on.

'Jaysus,' I said finally, 'poor old Nicholas. I was very
fond of him.'

'He was very fond of you,' she said, without irony.

'Was he?'

'He was, Jack,' she said.

I sighed, because suddenly it was a pleasure to be in the car, talking to her. Oh, a strange old world. An echo indeed of other days. Talking at our ease, like human persons. A person, especially a person that had married the other person, might be forgiven for missing that. But the hard truth was, Mai looked yellow, sickly, thinned away, with that curious false pregnancy about the stomach that gin will give. We rarely made love, it was true, what I lived on was merely the memory of her body – the intoxication that it had been to me, without any such crude assistance as alcohol. Just as I was thinking this, there was a gap in the clouds, and a big placard of sunlight threw itself across the avenue ahead of us. The old metal gates, unpainted this long while, the chilly-looking eagles on each pillar, and the unusual decrepitude of the grass either side of the avenue, were suddenly laid bare, illuminated, and in that moment something about Omard was betrayed: it had been gradually changing too, it too gradually making itself unreachable in the true sense. For some years now there had been no telegrams with 'mayfly up' urgently stencilled on them. And whatever the Sheridans had heard about us in Sligo, and I presumed given the nature of the country and its multitudes of ears and mouths ready to relay secrets and hidden things, they had heard most of our news, I also had heard news now and then about them, and how Nicholas's illness had weakened him, not to mention the horrors of the so-called economic war, when cattlemen like Nicholas, with no one to send their beef to, had been oftentimes obliged to kill their calves in the fields where they dropped.

Mai beside me started to laugh. It was scarifying laughter. She just sat there laughing for a few minutes and I didn't dare ask her at what.

After a while then she bid me drive on and we went up the winding mile of the avenue to the house. There was a little crowd of farm workers in their best bib and tucker, and a few black cars parked up on the lawn, and half a dozen pony and traps, and a couple of fancier gigs of some ancient design, and clumps of friends and remnant family, and just as we reached the semicircular carriage-turn before the front door, whose gravel unlike in former days was unraked and overgrown with grass, out came six men in dark suits carrying the coffin, with Maria a seventh figure behind, looking more rotund, more silent, and much older, as if myself and Mai had not seen her for twenty years, rather than the ten years or so that had intervened. Mai hurriedly opened the car door and went quickly over to her, holding the smaller woman in an embrace, laying her heavily powdered cheek on Maria's shoulder, itself covered in a snowfall of dandruff, very clear and copious on the shiny old satin dress.

Maria herself died a month later and Omard was left to a nephew who showed no interest in the place. Indeed it was the ironical duty of the Land Commission to 'stripe' the land, after the nephew took the roof off the house to avoid the rates, and made no use of Nicholas's generous acres. I was thankful that that particular job didn't fall to me.

Everything had been said without saying a word, everything had been understood without any intimation of understanding.

Dr Snow had twined himself around the falling tree that was Mai, and was growing on her like ivy – that was my understanding of it anyhow. Dr Snow was said to be a bit of a Lothario. He inspired a great devotion in some of his women patients anyway. Maybe I wasn't seeing things with clarity, but I didn't trust him, traipsing in and out, ministering to her, and a wonderful bill being run up as well. In came the gin bottles too somehow or other, not via Dr Snow of course, but more mysteriously. I am inclined to believe that Gaffney's delivered to the back gate under cover of darkness. Then up the stairs they went somehow to her bedroom.

It was the fleet footstep of Dr Snow twice a week up the same stairs that used to give me pause. But I am telling myself now there was nothing in it. Perhaps the truth was he liked her and felt sorry for her.

I soon had cause to be glad of Dr Snow, because much to Mai's surprise, and mine, she fell pregnant once more. Late '38, early '39 maybe. Mai had thought she had a chest infection, pleurisy maybe, because she had a pain in her back. When Dr Snow told her what really ailed her, she sank down on her knees, such was the shock of it.

'I can't have another baby!' she said.

'Well,' said Dr Snow.

When my Mam congratulated her Mai just stared back at her. But then, bit by bit, she seemed to be reconciled to it. She began to see the funny side of it. We had occasionally ended up in the bed together, certainly, but still, this was bordering on the miraculous. She said she'd be writing a letter to the Holy Ghost to complain. She didn't say that to Father Gaunt or my mother of course. It was our private joke.

It was in the same year the war began in Europe. It was as if a wraith had become pregnant, and it needed all Dr Snow's delicate knowledge to get her through. It was a beautiful spring. The two children were loosed into the street itself and ancient traditional games were reinvented in a thrice as is in the gift of children.

Mai took a continuous fancy to knocking about with me again, and when I wasn't traversing the complicated and contentious acres of my district for the Land

Commission, I would ferry her to the Rosses, where she might walk in her gravid state along the fringe of the shore. She was talkative in a way I hardly remembered, even in the early days. The twice-weekly visits to the cinema were religiously resumed. Fred Astaire, formerly her emperor and her god, crept back into her conversation. She suddenly had life in her, and was in the process of giving life to another, and something about this pregnancy was very different from the others, as if the years of drinking in her room were a long preparation for an almost holy sobriety now. She was not even herself, or herself restored, it was a new self.

Kipling's stories are buoyant, but sometimes buoyant on a very dark sea. If something is sad in a way that does not hurt, I will openly cry as I read a book, I don't see any shame in that. But my own story is making me sad. It is hurting me, here under the Accra sky.

I don't feel like myself, or rather, my self. 'I'm not myself,' we say, but what does it mean? Until I began to write everything down I didn't have the slightest notion what it purported to mean. Maybe now when I think I am understanding, I am instead mistaking everything, but at least I am perceiving something in the place of the great fog that has persisted through my life. A fog that no light apparently could properly pierce. There is a great mountain, and high ravines, and great danger, but the fog says nothing about that, the fog only talks on and on about itself. It is not interested in any fashion in clarity, naturally. But now and then, the fog disperses, and in little gloamings of clear light I seem to see the figures, my parents, Mai, my children, standing or sitting, talking, prosecuting you might say their lives and days. Continuing. But I am now at a great disadvantage too, because what is filling me, like rain in a low meadow without proper drainage, is sorrow, a fierce and hurtful sorrow. Hurtful. I would ask God, and if not God, a beneficent-minded angel, for some answer as to why Mai Kirwan had such a fate as hers, why she among all the people, all the women of the world, was assigned that fate, when to begin with she was so full of promise and laden indeed with gifts. Who was one of the brightest instances of womankind in the Galway of her youth, who seemed to be a person that might do anything, go anywhere, be anything she liked. So why was this bleak fate assigned? It is inexplicable, unless God or his deputy angel knows why, and of course He is saying nothing, and his angel is keeping mum also.

A ball of wool so knotted it could not be resolved, the knots pulled tighter and tighter. I see it better now but this enlightenment does not bring happiness. It does bring a sort of cold certainty, that I might even associate with the courage of the soldier, when a great cataclysm of bomb or army is upon him, and he finds himself not as terrified as he imagined he would be, but unexpectedly resigned and ready – poised for heroism and even death.

Because, it is terrible to me that in that time of her pregnancy, when the usually unhelpful environs of Sligo itself seemed to conspire with her, the white heather replacing the snow on Knocknarea, then the sun all summer long pouring yellow light into the cups and bowls of the land, and every Sligo child was roasted red on the strands, the human creature mirroring that strange weather in her own strange heart, when the gin was not for that term her mysterious companion, and when, despite everything, she turned to me as if I might be again, or even for the first time, her husband and her friend, that these efforts, these manifestations of the ability of the human soul to recover, to begin again, just as the child may innocently invent again the old game so oft invented, were met only with the poor hand and dour face of tragedy.

Our child was born dead. It is not feasible for a nondrinking man to write those words, but I have written them anyway. I don't know what to do. The rain falls on the roof like dancers, dancing there in two hundred hobnailed boots. Colin, a little scrap we put in his swaddling clothes and buried in a grave belonging to my father in Sligo cemetery. In early winter, when the ground was beginning to be resistant to the spade. When the gravedigger gets an intimation of the hardship awaiting him in the frozen months, should there be more deaths. When the day begins to lack its proper freight of hours. When, in that instance of our ill luck, it seemed there was more cruelty than joy stored up in the human story, and kindness and comfort only rationed, and the ration book for both indeed not issued to everyone. An hour when the bell of the cathedral sounded in the lower town with a fantastical and overwhelming meaning. When the mother stood there without her child. When the father stood without his son.

Maggie and Ursula were sad as owls. I would always try to read to them before bed, on my tour of their two small rooms under the roof, and now all the more assiduously, trying to hold onto normal things. Normal things are the hardest to hold onto, in my experience. *The Tale of Mrs Tiggy-Winkle.* Sally Henny-penny looking for her long yellow gloves. Lucy walking so high above the town she might throw a pebble down a chimney. The thimble filling under the waterfall, the robin's red waistcoat in the laundry basket.

But soon after Colin died, Maggie banished me from the edge of her bed. When you lose these little dispensations you see them for the house-high boons they are. And so I carried my book to Ursula only.

It was the loss of those small things also then to make you cry.

I was so sad about Colin I didn't pay enough attention to what was happening to Tom and Roseanne. But there was a dark kerfuffle there. Roseanne somehow going off the rails, meeting some bowsie on the top of Knocknarea mountain. But other things too. Tom so shocked and hurt, and the Mam moving then to disencumber him of Roseanne, that's the only word for it. Mam's hero Father Gaunt weighing in to help, said he would work for an annulment in Rome. Poor Roseanne put into the old tin hut in Strandhill that Tom formerly used to store things for his dancehall. Like she was a broken chair. I went out there myself with Father Gaunt to try and explain things to her. Dreadful commission. But she didn't seem to understand, she didn't seem to be thinking clearly, not at all.

A dark business. A dark time, indeed.

Then the war came, swallowing suddenly, in one great gulp, these smaller matters, the ground of the world opening, and everything pouring down through it.

Chapter Seventeen

I spent a couple of weeks trying to settle our affairs. Then I was going to join up. I was thirty-seven, which is old for a soldier, but the army was looking for engineers and the like. My reasons were obscure to me, but I knew I would do it. My first idea was to get Mai and the girls out of Ireland, because everyone seemed to think the Germans would invade immediately, as a way of getting to England. Or that Churchill would invade instead, and bring the war onto us that way. De Valera was weaving and ducking in a dance of neutrality which seemed doomed to speedy failure. So I asked around and someone told me that Malta would be a good bet, that no one would bother with Malta, and there were houses going there for the price of a Sligo henhouse. So I put Magheraboy on the market and sold it to a lad from Bonniconlon, and much to my relief Mai seemed to go along with the Malta idea. I managed to purchase a house there through an agency in Dublin. Then we packed up everything you could take in an Austin motorcar. The children were in the car, bursting with excitement, and I went back to fetch Mai, and pull the hall door closed. She was standing in the hall, shaking.

'I can't go, Jack,' she said. 'I'm sorry.'

'But Mai, we're all packed.'

She shook her head, as if there were invisible bonds tying her to the floor, her face so uncertain, so betwixt and between, I felt terribly sorry for her. She had been through hell and the record of that journey was written on her face. But I was angry too, angry, Jesus, Mary and St Joseph.

I resold the Malta house, whatever it had looked like, I never even saw a photograph of it, and in great haste found a place in Finisklin, the former premises of the harbourmaster. So instead of driving from Sligo to Malta, via many a ship and unknown way, we drove from Sligo to Sligo, and unpacked our goods and chattels in an old stone house by the river.

1940. Tom had driven up from Sligo to Ballycastle with the girls so they could 'see their father in his new get-up'. We met in a little seaside hotel. Beyond the grimy windows lay Rathlin Island, like a hunting dog asleep on the sea. My temporary commission was just in the offing, and my officer training nearly at an end. I had been away from home for five or six months.

'Well, Jack,' said Tom, 'there you are, in all your finery.'

'Aye,' I said.

'I suppose you know ten years ago you'd have been shot for wearing that garb,' he said, smiling.

'Arra,' I said.

'If the British want to invade Ireland you can tell them they can cross the border at Belcoo. By Jesus, there wasn't a soul to stand in our way.'

'Ah, sure,' I said.

'And I had the children hiding in the back seat.'

'Ah, sure, they don't mind you coming over, Tom. Sure haven't you played Ballycastle often enough with the band?'

'Jesus, I have, in happier times.'

Then we settled in to drink some tea and I gave Maggie a few tanners to buy lollipops if there were still such things in the world, and she herded the smaller one out onto the wharf.

'Don't be falling into the water now,' I said.

We talked about nothing then as people do, and then we ran out of nothing.

'It's nice of you to drive them over,' I said.

'It's a long time not to see their father,' he said, and in my private mind I said *uh-oh*, here it comes.

'I don't need to tell you there's been difficulties since you left,' he said, and seemed to get stuck immediately.

'What difficulties, Tom?' I said.

'Well, I suppose I don't need to say anything about the heart of the matter. Is there any chance you might get back to see her, you know? Mai, I mean.'

'Well, I'm not due leave for a bit anyhow.'

'That's a pity then,' he said.

'I know,' I said.

'Mai's in the doss mostly and Mam says she's just crying most of the day.'

I sat there in silence for a moment, withdrawing my legs a little.

'How's Roseanne getting on?' I said.

'There's talk of getting her into the asylum, you know.'

'Jesus, how do things get so bad? You'd have to ask.'

'Well, it has my heart broken, let me tell you.'

'It's a terrible business, Tom.'

'Ah, Jesus,' said Tom, 'this marriage business. Did anyone tell us it would be so bloody tricky?'

'I don't remember anyone telling us,' I said.

I sensed he wanted to go now. Maybe he was just on a mission for the Mam. But still, he had come all that way. Smuggling the girls across into the bargain.

'I hope those children haven't gone and drowned themselves,' he said.

'Well, haven't you the two medals for the life-saving, Tom?' I said, and indeed he had, one of them for pulling Roseanne from the sea years ago when she got into trouble. A young woman of unfathomable beauty nearly drowned in the fathoms themselves. Strandhill beach. 'Earl Grey, and a dead-fly bun,' I used to say to her, when she was just a girleen in the Café Cairo. I was forgetting things about normal life. I was forgetting ordinary things. Mai had been a divil for the Earl Grey too. In happier times.

'Damme, I do,' he said, laughing. 'Two bloody medals.' Nice, round, friendly Tom, I thought, on a mercy mission to Ballycastle, in the middle of a world war.

'Take them to the Giant's Causeway on the way back,' I said. 'Sure they'll love that.'

'I will,' said Tom, 'I will. Good idea.'

The colonel listened to my account of my wife's distress and granted me compassionate leave. I was surprised and apprehensive in the same breath. I didn't know how much of that he read in my face.

'We'll have time enough to make proper use of you, McNulty,' he said.

In Derry as I swept through I bought her a bracelet with rubies – worthy of an officer's wife, I was thinking. I had the strength of character to scorn the garnets anyhow. I drove over the border to Donegal still in my uniform, somewhat in defiance of the recent law against wearing such garb in Eire. I understood why De Valera wanted the country to stay neutral, he was afraid the place would erupt in civil war again if he so much as allowed one British battleship into an Irish harbour, but I didn't agree with him when it came to not being allowed to show the pride I felt in my undertaking as a soldier. Indeed, I passed across the border as if there was no border between the North and South, just as Tom had said. As if there was a secret unity between the two places – the secret unity of that bloody awkward, ferociously demanding thing called daily life.

I bought the bracelet because I still loved her. That is the bare fact of it. However much I feared our life together, and I did fear it, the chaos sometimes, and the hurt, now I was boundlessly eager to see her. I wanted her to be different, and absolutely the same. I wanted the same dust to be lingering on the furniture in the bedroom in Harbour House and I wanted a new broom of grace and usefulness to wipe everything clean.

When I got to the house I thought I might have been granted my strange wish. She or someone anyhow had washed winter from the door and the five staring windows at the front of the house shone with polished cleanliness, and sparkled back at the whale-coloured waters of the Garvoge hurrying past. Across the river the remnant town lay in a fierce scratched line of dark ink and pencil. A motorcar turning somewhere distantly against the weak sunlight threw out a cold plaque of light briefly on the tumbling water. A cargo ship took its course between the deep-water bollards, burning with softened light like a huge floating ember. I saw the rage of weeds and grass in our bit of garden across the road, with its toppling arched gate, and suddenly I could see myself in there, in some undetermined future, with a spade, turning the sods, laying out the rows for potatoes, carrots and cabbages, in old clothes specially kept for the purpose. I hesitated, staring at all this, past, present and future in a tumble of old light, with my hand on the latch and the key inserted in the lock. Happiness and fear invaded me – the cocktail of wartime.

The interior had that scant look of the drinker's house right enough, when so many articles, old dinner plates and servers, have been smashed in so many arguments and fumbling, flustered wars, and only a selection of the objects that might decorate a dwelling are on view, as if many things have been packed away carefully in trunks and boxes, or, as in our case, shoved into bins over the years in cascades of shattered delph, the archaeology and remnant grandeur of her father's life. The mezzotint of that same grandee was in the hall, that had been in her bedroom at Magheraboy, beside the one of her mother in a Victorian gossamer dress, with her permanent look of worried defiance.

Everything otherwise was as it should be. As it should be and so rarely was. The carpets, brushmarks of Persian weaving, were worn but had the look of having been recently beaten. Someone had swept the floorboards and the linoleum, someone had polished the surface of the bockety hall table – one of the feet missing its ivory wheel. Now here was the open door into the sitting room, and here was Mai coming out, looking very springlike and coiffured in her best silk dress. There was a little yellowness about the gills, but she had obviously spent a long time sitting at her dressing table, smoothing out her face with make-up, and choosing the right lipstick for her complexion. And the thing most rare of all in recent times, she was smiling.

She came right up to me and laid her head on my khaki chest. I hadn't put down my valises and wished heartily that I had but did not wish simply to drop them at our feet or ask her to let me put them down because I wanted to embrace her gently – I thought I might never get her back at my chest again if I said or did anything.

'Oh Jack, dear Jack,' she said.

Chapter Eighteen

It didn't last of course, it couldn't have. I think she thought I was coming back for good, that I had found some way out of the army, at Tom's request maybe, or that some hidden clause had been uncovered and invoked. It wasn't so good when I had to remind her that I had signed up for the duration of the war. But the war I said mightn't last long, and then I would be back, right as rain, and we could pick everything up. I said I might be able to stay in the army, that promotion came quickly oftentimes in wartime, and we might find ourselves stationed somewhere nice, in peacetime, maybe even England, and then she could maybe find work as a teacher if she so wished, as her married state would not be a bar to that there. And she made an enormous and obvious effort to listen with a good grace. I suppose I could see now that her nerves, as Queenie had put it, were not good, not good at all. And that if they had been good, the death of our little boy had set her back.

That night, after a few gins, she whispered to me in the first friendliness of drunkenness that she had not been feeling well, not well at all, that Queenie didn't understand and Jack Kirwan had made a ghost of himself in her life, he wouldn't or couldn't come to her. That there was a terror in her, a terror she did not know the name of. That it scampered through her veins like a rat and took away from her every semblance of peace or enjoyment. That her head, her very head, was heavy with pain, as if it were a pail of poison. And then after a few more gins, slowly slowly it all became my fault, and in the deep of the night she threw the old wall clock at my head, and then she threw the cat, having nothing else at hand, and I drank till I was dizzy, and in the morning, waking alone in the sitting room, I wandered out into the hall, and found Ursula at the foot of the stairs, staring at the body of her mother where she had fallen, sometime in the lost hours of the night, neither an angel from heaven, nor a demon risen from the earth, but a human and tormented soul.

When I got back to Ballycastle I found the ruby bracelet forgotten in my inside pocket, and so was obliged, rather mournfully, to post it.

Outside in the yard, in one of those queer little gaps between downpours, some nameless blue bird is singing with immense sweetness. I am staring at a photo of Mai and the children that I carry in my wallet. I am not in the picture myself, possibly because I am taking it. It is around this time it was taken, judging by the size of Maggie, although she was always a tall child. In which case the reason I am not in it might be not because I am taking the photo but because I am away at the war. They both look well turned out, Mai herself quite trim. She's wearing sunglasses like a jazz musician, but there is no sun. Her stern, unsmiling expression doesn't say much about anything, but her clothes have been put on with care. Somehow it makes me rather stupidly sad, as if it is a photo of what might have been even though it is an actual photo of what was. Maybe Ursula looks a bit cold in her gansaí, and her hair with that dry, dead look hair gets when there are nits in it. That may be fanciful of me, and maybe not. Both of the girls had nits from time to time. It was the great era of the head-louse.

I had to leave her to it. That is not an easy thing to think of. None of it is easy to think of. As a young man of sixteen, seventeen, before I went to the university, the First World War just finishing, the seas heaving still with mines, in my beautiful white uniform, a wireless officer with the face of a child, proud as Punch, I saw every port of the earth, yes, and rounded Cape Horn a dozen times in tempests and in resplendent calms, I saw evil dens and heard dark talk, and knew the world was not entirely a pleasant place, as you hope it might be when you are young, setting out for the first time to seek your fortune. Bleak streets of Bombay and Liverpool, men who didn't care if they lived or died, and would blithely stick you with a knife as they themselves slid down into hell. But none of those things ever struck me with the overwhelming force of Mai's allotted fate. I wrote something like this a few days ago, I am writing it again today. I still don't understand, really, what language it is told in properly, or what place, truly, it describes. The Arabs say everything is already written and that we've got to fulfil the book. What darkness, what vileness, what a tome blacked out with blackest ink, was tendered to Mai. And she was obliged, day by day, paragraph by paragraph, chapter by chapter, to live it. My mind withers at the thought just as it shrinks from the task of remembering these fragments of it now, and struggles to find light.

My first job after getting my commission was to help bolster British Africa against possible French invasion, as I have already described. In Accra after my ship was torpedoed, they hospitalised me and a hundred other rescued soldiers. Many, many others had been lost in the attack or drowned in the sea. My body, somewhat to my surprise, because I thought I had come through 'unscathed' as they say, was marked with bruises like a strange map of a new world, the seas and oceans my unmarked skin, the bruises, red and black, the unknown landmasses with their deceptive harbours. The ward sister was a little Irish nun with a heart as big as the Sahara, and as warm, and her African nurses were joyful, pretty and adroit. She was of the opinion that it was the whisky I had drunk had saved me. Perhaps she meant it humorously. I healed, and when I was let out of hospital after a couple of months, I found myself seconded as an engineer to a unit of the Gold Coast Regiment. Everyone was still thinking that the Vichy French might invade, though it was a thought that was fading. The looming danger dissolving in the acid of what actually was fated to happen, that no one, not the brightest general or statesman, really knows.

I was bussed up to Asante country, feeling every rut in the road, staring out at the queer procession of epic landscape, lovely distant hills with soft greens marked on them by the subtlest touch of the brush, and then narrow treed-in fields, where children ran screaming alongside the truck like dark river-stones turned over and over by a current. I was headed for the old town of Kumasi. My rank by then was already first lieutenant, and when I came into barracks there was some confusion, because apparently there was already a man there of the same rank and name.

'You are already here, sir,' said the quartermaster, a small bronze-coloured man. His cheeks were marked by old knife cuts like the shallow ruts on Brazil nuts.

'Well, I don't know what to say about that,' I said.

'The mess sergeant already served you, sir, last night, look, sir, I have it on the mess sheet. First Lieutenant John Charles McNulty.'

'And did you meet me yesterday yourself?' I said.

'I did, sir, and I can tell you, it was not you, sir.'

But he was laughing of course. Nevertheless this was verging on miracle and mystery, and I was intrigued and a small bit discombobulated. It is not a stable thought to be suddenly two in the world when you were sure you had only been one.

Then I had a strange meeting in the officers' quarters. The beds were narrow and metal, not in any way better than what the ordinary soldiers had. A democratic barracks, such as you find now and then in the army overseas. The quartermaster brought me along to meet a long, skinny man lounging on a bed, or at least one third of him lounging and the rest sticking out onto the floor. I could see him glancing at my cap to see how he should address me, but we were the same rank right enough. I noted he wasn't in the sappers, but in a tank corps.

He was immensely friendly and quite happy to meet me. We went for a stroll about the camp, then took refuge from the roasting heat in the commandant's office, the only place with a man working a cooling fan. We laughed a bit, and he asked me about my experiences getting up to Kumasi, and was very interested to hear about the torpedoed ship. I knew he knew my name and he knew I knew his name, and maybe for a moment he tried to imagine himself, First Lieutenant John Charles McNulty, roiling about in the murderous waters. I could tell he was a bit of a toff, and by something he said about something else, I opined he was from Ireland also, and then by something else he said that he was from Sligo, and then, in the coarse gravelly heat of the Gold Coast, my head felt all the dizzier, wondering how this could be.

So we talked further, and he mentioned his home place, an old estate I knew from seeing its granite gates when you passed in a car on the road to Enniscrone. Then I felt the blood leaving my cheeks, and the air deserting my gills. I was seized for a moment by something as close to a heart attack as I ever want to experience. It was a ludicrous reaction. As a little child I had of course believed my father's stories like a Christian believes the Bible. And when I got older, I told myself I believed them, and made an act of faith in them, but all underneath that was doubt and disbelief and faithlessness. In particular, the unlikely old tale of a dispossessed brother in the seventeenth century, similar to a thousand old tales in a thousand Irish families. But now, from everything this man said, the story was being validated, inch by inch and line by line. The man before me was the descendant of a brother of the Oliver McNulty that my father had often spoken of. Oh, yes, he said, it is all in the family archive. This was spoken in the most amicable, even regretful way, in his English accent from his schooling at Eton, while I stood before him dumbfounded and halting in speech.

We shook hands over a little rickety table of papers, containing I would imagine the plans to blow all the bridges in that district if the French looked like coming to take it. I gave him my version of the story, as if before a strange court where we were obliged to say truthfully who we were, as if we could ever know such a thing before God or man, who I was, or who I imagined I was, and the other First Lieutenant John Charles McNulty nodded enthusiastically at my shadowy story, and then he gripped my hand. There was no trace of a family likeness, but to the quartermaster, standing on the edge of this and listening, it must have seemed odd that these two men had never met, the same age and from the same town, and with the same name. But then the quartermaster could not be expected to understand the lives of Catholic and Protestant souls in Irish provincial towns.

'Yes,' he said, with solemnity, 'we know who we are, you and I.'

That night we tore into the whisky without mercy and

cancelled out everything, stars and old stories and the electric radio of the insects, the spinning mess room and the other young officers. Our stories dissolved in the happy chaos of the alcohol, someone must have carried us to our beds, First Lieutenant John Charles McNulty and First Lieutenant John Charles McNulty. He was due out at 0400 hours the next morning, I heard him go, and I never saw him again.

Chapter Nineteen

Furlough. It was the snow I remember as the first thing, a crumbly, thick fall of it, as if the whole of Sligo was turned into a great hall just to contain the whim and majesty of that snow, with the roof too high and dark to see, the walls obscured by the consummate genius of those small, white flakes, with a music so silent you cocked an ear to it. I came up the Finisklin road slowly in the ancient taxi, a road by chance I had designed and overseen the building of some years before myself, for the town council, one of whose members was my brother Tom. Now that Great Labourer whose face is not known was quietly spreading this tonnage of white gravel as a curious and useless surface, and the tyres pressed it down as if it were white insects to be crushed, and the lamps saw only whiteness and bright darkness, and now and then opening and closing, short vales and copses of snowless air, where a house I knew might appear, the doctor's gates on the left, the deep black of the Garvoge mixing with the black Atlantic that had crept up on the tide, an ink so dark it was like a billion words printed over and over each other, the story of the world pushing up to the town bridge, the story of the world being sucked back down to Oyster Island and the Rosses, all unreadable, unknowable, cancelled out. The old Wolseley crept on. I heard the engine purring in the hood. I was anxious to reach home. Is this still 1940? – it's so hard to be precise, but I think it was after Africa, before London. I was heading for Harbour House of course, heading home. At the top of the road it would be standing, looking back towards Sligo, the river close there, scratching past the great stones of the wharf wall and the mid-water bollards, the Garvoge, a being so entirely capable and strong, wide, deep and dark, that it always seemed to me while we lived there as if it might pull away the town from its moorings, pull away the house, pull away the landscape like a strange carpet, the model school, and Middleton's fields, and my potato garden with its imperilled arch.

At last, still with the curious obligation of slowness, we reached the front of the house, with its pillared portico and five black windows, clean or grimy this time I could not make out, not a light in the place that I could see. And I climbed out of the car, leaving the warm squeak of the cracked leather seat, and shut the door with its genial click, paid old McCormack, and stepped carefully to the house in my engineer's boots. I opened my own front door, and went into the black hall with its brown linoleum and haggard table, pulled my coat off and cast it on a chair, and perched my hat on one of its wooden horns. Then I walked on down the dark corridor, wondering where everyone was, maybe thinking the little ones were asleep in the rooms above. I heard some sounds from the back of the house and went on further down, and was obliged to open the second door into our small garden. The light from a rear bedroom was trying to pierce the snowfall, and in the difficult muddle of the whiteness I saw two figures, Mai clearest in a black dress, and at her feet half lying and half risen, was the form of my daughter Ursula, who when I peered and peered I could see was in her nightshift, a small, pale person maybe nine or ten years old, and Mai with her right arm raised, and then letting it fall, her right arm raised, then letting it fall, and I stepped two feet out onto the pristine snow, which had already covered the tracks of my wife and her daughter, as if they had merely appeared in the centre of that bare garden, and I looked up at the window of light, something catching my eye, and saw in the glare of a lamp another standing, Maggie still and staring, as the dark arm rose and fell, rose and fell, with the switch gripped in the hand, that I could just see also, like a feathery line on an engraving, rising and falling, and Ursula silent, silent as a stone, and Mai panting, panting, I could hear her, as if she couldn't hit enough, as if she couldn't work hard enough at it, lashing and lashing the child, in the snow, in Sligo, in the darkness, and the snow falling, and nothing left in God's creation but that watching child, and the beaten child, and the ruined woman, and the consternated father.

'Mai, Mai!'

I rushed across the snow and got a hand on Mai's arm, to still it. Up to that moment I don't think she knew where she was, who she was. She stared at me in the muddled light. She must have forgotten I was due home, she must have forgotten a lot of things. I gathered up Ursula under an arm, registered the weight of her, and had to put my other arm around her too. For a moment I stood there with my daughter, just staring at my wife.

'What in the name of Jesus, Mai,' I said.

'Jack, Jack, is that you? Where did you spring from?' she said.

I carried Ursula into the cold house, wrapped her in a coverlet, and lit the fire in the sitting room, while the girl sat in a chair, sobbing. I rubbed her limbs to get some warmth back into her. I was inclined to sob myself. It was one thing to be at the war, trying to find a path through that, and another thing to be here, pathless, rudderless.

Then Mai came in from the garden and stood in the sitting room, not saying anything, very still, looking at me lighting the fire.

'Do you have matches, Mai?' I said.

'Yes, yes, I do,' she said, and went hurrying off to the kitchen maybe, to fetch them, coming back in with all the bustle and intent of a nurse.

'Has this child eaten anything?' I said.

'She got the stew, she got the stew,' said Mai.

'I'm going to bed her down here, and then we will go into the kitchen to talk,' I said. 'Don't you realise I have to go back tomorrow? I have only a day.'

'Only a day, Jack? Yes, yes, alright.'

Then we were in the freezing kitchen. There had been no housekeeping done for a while, that was for sure. Every plate we had was on the sink, every cup, every glass, every bit of cutlery. The place stank of bad meat and milk gone off.

'This is disgusting, Mai. What were you doing, out in the snow like that with Ursula?'

'She was being bold, Jack, being bold.'

'You wouldn't treat a dog like that.'

'Spare the rod and spoil the child, Jack.'

'Do you think? The child in her shift, in the bloody snow?'

'You're not here, Jack. They need their father here.'

'I am away at the war. Away at the war. The whole world is away at the war.'

'What the hell are you doing going out there?' she said. 'Nobody in Ireland gives a tuppenny damn about it.'

'When you see Hitler coming up Wine Street in a tank you might take a different view,' I said.

'Bloody Hitler – what did he ever do to you, Jack?'

'Mai!' I said, shouting now, because we were drifting off into the ancient topic of my culpability for everything. I felt a huge sense of emergency. I would have to go the next day, and I couldn't be thinking she would ever do what she had done again.

'If you ever go at Ursula like that again, so help me, Mai, I will kill you myself.'

'You will kill your own wife?'

'I will, Mai, in the most expedient manner I can think of.'

'You killed me already, Jack.'

'That *ochón is ochón ó* is no good now, Mai. That was for other days. Now I am telling you, you will not touch that child again. What sort of bloody foolishness is it, to be out in a yard, with a switch, beating and beating at her? Do you ever want to see heaven, Mai? There is no place in heaven for such a person.'

'You're not my priest, Jack, you're not my priest.'

'No, I am your husband, your unfortunate husband.'

'But you love me, Jack.'

Now she raised her face and looked at me squarely. There was a certain wild pride in her words. It was so strange. It was all so strange.

'There are limits to everything, even love. Not love for

a child, there are no limits to that. But love for a wife, now, maybe I am thinking there are some limits to that.'

'Why are you at that war, Jack?'

And then she was weeping, weeping. Maggie streeled in and stood behind her mother's legs.

'Maggie, dear, come here, and give your father a kiss,' I said, not expecting she would. But I thought I had to keep on saying the old things, the old things that didn't get old the way some old things did.

But she came around her mother and crossed the cold flags to me and gave me a kiss right enough.

'You must answer my letters when you get a chance. Did you keep all the stamps?'

Before I went away again, I brought Ursula over to the Mam's house and deposited her there. I said she was to live there till I got home, or the war was over. My mother asked me nothing about the marks the switch had left on Ursula's side. But she nodded sagely enough. I asked her had she heard anything of Eneas, and she said she had got a soldier's postcard from France. Then I kissed her and Ursula and said I had to be away again.

I marched back to Harbour House and asked Mai to do her best to pull herself together. I asked her to stop the drinking forthwith. She promised solemnly she would. I said she must apologise to Ursula, she must find some way to make amends. I could see she was very frightened, not by anything that was going to happen to her, but by what had happened. For myself, I could only wonder at her – was this a sort of evil borrowed from alcohol? I didn't believe that in herself, in her heart and soul, she was a vicious woman. How is it that for some people drinking is a short-term loan on the spirit, but for others a heavy mortgage on the soul? How is it many a drinker becomes gay and light-hearted, but some so darkly morose and rescinded, filleted of every scrap of happiness, that they might beat their child in the snow? I couldn't answer these questions then, and I can't answer them now. I took the risk of embracing Mai, and told her that I loved her. She looked defeated by the news. It was with a heavy heart and a feeling of dread that I went off again about the business of the war.

Chapter Twenty

I shunted myself to England, as my orders bid me, and was assigned to a unit in bomb disposal. I didn't know if I wanted to be in bomb disposal but at the same time didn't know much about it either.

I did a four-day course. Hitler had started to drop thousands of bombs on London, among which were many unexploded bombs. So we would be sent to defuse them. It's a tricky thing to be learning your trade off a big, mean-looking yoke that could blow you to kingdom come.

My sappers would dig to find it. Unexploded bombs had a habit of boring into the earth as far down as thirty feet. And they would veer about, depending on the ground, and end up not quite where you would expect. So my knowledge of geology came in handy. I would push down a long thin spike as the sappers dug, and hope finally to feel metal on metal. Then we could really scare ourselves, uncovering the sullen-looking thing, and checking it wasn't ticking or lying on its fuze.

Those were lovely boys, the sappers in my little unit. Pat Millane was a lad from the Aran islands.

'I don't tell them what I'm doing at home, sir,' he said. 'They think going off to war is a load of old billy goats' balls.'

Things like this he would say in Gaelic, privately to me, as it were. *Magalraí pocaide* is the Irish for billy goats' balls.

After my sappers dug out the hole, it was me on my own going down the ladder then and trying to get the fuze or fuzes out. Sometimes, in the boiling sweat of such occasions, I forgot about Mai. I forgot about everything, except the bomb I was sitting on. You used to sit on the bombs when you were drawing the fuze out, because in that way you wouldn't know a thing about it if it went up.

They had these fairly common jobs, (15)s they called them, that was the number the Germans would have marked on them. Their pilots had to know the numbers themselves, so the bombs could be armed properly before they dropped them. And later we began to find (17)s, which were tricky, because there was a booby trap under the main gaine, and when you had one of those coupled with a (50), which was motion-sensitive, well, at first people said nothing could be done then, only wait till the (50) deteriorated, or the bomb exploded, which was not always possible. Then the poor benighted BD men had to do their best, whatever was put in front of us, and the divil take the hindmost – which the divil was sometimes only too happy to do. When a man was blown up, you might only get a pound of flesh left of him, or a bit of an arm, or maybe a ruined cap – and that's what went into the coffin, and they'd weigh the rest of it down with sandbags, so the relatives wouldn't know. We knew all about that.

So that's why sometimes even Mai was driven from my thoughts. Then she would drift back in. I would wonder how Ursula and Maggie were getting on. Then we would be off again on some job, bumping through the streets of London in our BD truck.

We all saw terrible things. We were at the 'terrible things' end of things. I defused bombs, fifty kilos, 250, five hundred, a thousand, and those huge bombs, the parachute mines, in the very different geologies of the East End or the West End, and Bloomsbury, and the Isle of Dogs – all points of the compass.

Something shrank in us all the while, and something also grew in its place. It was thoughts of the possible future shrank. It was a sort of confidence in the nature of other people, the nature of the inhabitants of England mostly, that grew. BD men as time went on were appreciated. You got free drink in pubs when they saw the bomb insignia. Yellow and red, a little bomb on your shoulder, designed by Queen Mary herself.

Because you couldn't be thinking about the future. It was a cure for the present, any ills of the present. In a strange way it allowed me to survive my worries about Mai and the girls.

As an officer I was called sir, but that was the only real difference between us. There was a chivalry in the fact that only an officer would defuse a bomb, the sappers standing back behind a wall, when the digging was done. Many had their arses blown out through their mouths. Temporary gentlemen indeed.

I knew some BD officers who never told their wives what they did. I never told Mai about that particular tour of duty. She had enough on her plate.

Eventually Hitler seemed to get tired of trying to exterminate the citizenry of Britain – the spectacular citizenry – and hauled everything round and pointed himself towards Russia.

So I did a little stint in North Africa, not too far from where our ship had docked, years and years before, when me and Mai were just married.

I was moving with my unit of engineers across a ragged district. I suppose it must have been very early '42. We were destroying our own arms caches as quickly as we could, so that Rommel wouldn't have the good of them when he came through. His army was likely not far off, so we were nervy and watchful.

One evening we came to a few nondescript acres of desert. There was nothing marked on my map to say there had been an engagement here. But there were shattered creatures of metal that had once been British and German tanks, and here and there in fierce decay the bodies of fallen men, burned out of their vehicles and then killed, and infantry killed as they moved forward. I stood there, gazing at this aftermath of a nameless battle, now maybe a month or two old. I couldn't tell if we had won or lost the encounter, and the attitudes of the dead seemed to say that that was of no importance. All were dead and their nationality was not now of this earth.

I had climbed down off the transport to see if I could identify our soldiers, and my living soldiers were watching me from the covered truck, subdued and silent. Now I turned on my heel to go back to them.

A lark, a single bird with her dowdy plumage, burst up from her cup of sand just in front of me and like a needle flashing in my mother's hand of old made a long stitch between earth and heaven, with a joyousness that rent my heart.

I was writing as often as I could to Maggie and Ursula. Maggie never answered or her letters were lost, but Ursula's many letters followed me about. It was always news of her grandparents, humorous in nature. She especially loved Pappy. There was no talk of Mai.

Anyway I was swung back their way on my next posting, which was a return to Ballycastle to be liaison officer to the Yanks coming in for training.

Of course Ballycastle was already part of the great empire of dancing in Ireland. But nothing quite prepared it for the black GIs. The soldiers aglow with energy, and the Ballycastle women on fire with enthusiasm, thrown into the air, sliding down backs, their skirts lifting and falling. Ordinary Irishmen could only stand by in resignation. They arranged themselves on Ballycastle Strand, dotting the little rocky coves. Kitted out in their greatcoats, they gazed with wonder at the local people getting into the arctic water. Far from causing scandal to the folk of Ballycastle, it was their white officers who were alarmed and affronted. Of course there was segregation at home but Ballycastle people didn't care about that.

'Captain,' one of the American lieutenants implored me, 'we got to do something about this.'

As liaison officer I heard a good deal about it. Little booklets were given out. You'd see them thrown into the gutters like so many unwanted sand-dabs.

'We got to do something, captain.'

I thought we had a better chance of winning the bloody war with them coming into it.

I was trying to plot a way to break the impasse for Mai. I talked to the army doctor about cures, because it was a big problem in the forces, and he was an expert in drying out and other matters.

'I should see if I couldn't get her into hospital for a while,' he said. 'Just the absence of drink would be very beneficial. She might start to see things in a clearer light.'

On my next furlough, I was hopeful.

Strangely enough, Mai *was* in hospital when I got back. But it was with illness, her lungs were stuck to her backbone with pleurisy, and I knew immediately she had not been taking care of herself. There wasn't much surprise in that, but it was very upsetting. Mam had Maggie now as well as Ursula, getting the meals into them, and shunting them to school in the Ursuline convent.

I asked Dr Snow about the drinking, whether he could get her dry now in the hospital, and he looked at me as if I were daft.

'She is dry,' he said. 'You can do a lot of things in an Irish hospital, I am sure, but drinking's not one of them, as far as I'm aware.'

'Well, that's good,' I said.

'She was a week in the house barely able to move, your

daughter finally came to fetch me. We're lucky she didn't die,' he said.

'It's bloody tricky,' I said, 'because I'm in the army, you know.'

'Yes,' he said. 'I know. Listen, Mr McNulty, since you raise the issue of her drinking, might I just make the observation that your own drinking is very considerable, and not a help to her, especially if you would like her to stop.'

'Well, I only drink socially, to be sociable,' I said, to my discredit. I think I must call that a lie. Dr Snow didn't, though I suspected he would have liked to.

'We had best leave her be for the moment,' he said, 'and try and get her better. Then we can think about the other thing.'

'By all means,' I said.

'How long do you have for leave?'

'I'm due back tomorrow night.'

'They keep you busy in the army then,' he said.

Chapter Twenty-one

I found myself catapulted over to Yorkshire to teach bomb disposal. I was drinking heavily, and I think my superior officers may have been relieved to be rid of me, though they didn't quite say so. But the camp in Yorkshire was glad to see me, because on paper I was an expert. And indeed I *was* an expert.

Pat Millane was up there too, as it happened. He was assigned to help me with the demonstrations. My students were gleaming young officers. We worked in a big old barn, out of the Yorkshire weather. The oak-beam roof was very beautiful, enough to warm an engineer's heart. There was plenty of room to line up all the bombs, and all the fuzes and gear, and Pat had managed to nab a big boiler to show how to steam out explosive, and all the latest contraptions to remove a fuze mechanically were at hand.

It was very strange to be working in perfect safety.

There was a room annexed to the barn that was our mess, where you could get a pint or two between classes.

The young officers were very eager. I can still see their faces peering at me as I instructed them.

One day we were spending a long afternoon demonstrating the subtle guile of the parachute bomb. We had a hollow example of this nine-foot horror. The fuzes were a (17) and a (50), and we were demonstrating the usefulness of making the mine believe it was underwater. The bombs were first used as sea-mines, and they were primed to explode as they hit water, or failing that, to sink a number of feet and then to explode. But if it sank deeper, the fuze would shut itself down, and wait instead for a ship to pass overhead, when the mechanism would be prompted back to life. But these bombs began also to be dropped onto cities. So some clever man had devised the use of a rubber bladder off a bicycle horn, and a tube, and a bicycle pump, and the trick was to convince the fuze that it had dropped to a certain depth, so that it would shut off. Air was forced into the fuze to imitate water pressure. The trouble then was, the slightest knock would set its clock going again, and it had been discovered that the fuze would explode the mine after just seventeen seconds, which is no time at all, and this was what I was trying to teach my student officers.

So we devised a little game, which was to try and hoodwink the fuze, officer by officer. We had the harmless mine hanging from the rafters by ropes to imitate the parachute, as these bombs often snagged on chimneys and the like, as they plummeted down through houses. My officers were fabulously alive to the task, and even though we knew in our hearts we were working in safety, nevertheless a tremendous tension built up, as one by one they attached the ridiculous-looking tube and pump and rubber blister, and listened for the sound of the clock stopping, and in ever more dreadful silence for the sound of it popping back into life. The first two men managed pretty well. The third brushed the mine just as he got it quiet, and he heard the little clock starting again. Then we fled, scattering to the four corners of the barn, just to see how far a soul could get in seventeen seconds, but also, in a queer way, half believing by now that the bomb really would explode.

And then nothing of course, the seven of us standing at the fringes of the barn, in the strangest silence, until I started to laugh, and then the others laughed, the voices a bit higher than usual, just a touch of hysteria, and the man who had knocked his knee against the mine was shaking, shaking with silence, and then with laughter also, and all of us laughing then, like proper eejits, but living eejits.

So I called a break in our efforts and deemed it a good time to have a drink in the mess and we could go back then and have another try. And I was feeling rather stupidly satisfied with myself, and as always thought I could tell this story to Mai at home, when I got there, and maybe it would be something to cheer her up, or maybe not, maybe not say anything, maybe that was always the best stratagem. I ordered two pints for myself, the other officers ordered just the one.

Then the lads had downed their beer and it was time to return.

We were stationed not far from an RAF camp and I heard in the distance an airplane returning to base. It was late afternoon but still daylight so I assumed the aircraft was on some routine run over its own territory. The young officers trooped back into the barn through the narrow wooden door, and I gripped the glass that held my second pint, intending to swallow it down as quickly as I could. I was even a bit relieved that they wouldn't be there to see me, as in my heart of hearts I felt it was a little greedy, the greed of the hapless drinker. Which I was still able to disapprove of, with the curious double self of the drinker. The only witness now was the pleasant mess-man, Corporal Timmony. I was still half aware of the plane engine in the distance, or rather, nearer now, and in the same instant, Corporal Timmony looked at me, and I looked at him, and I suspect we had the same thought, the exact same thought, or rather question in our minds, but how ridiculous, broad daylight, only one in ten thousand German planes tried anything in daylight, but of course, Hull was not too far off, and all the factories of the Humber, maybe it was a lone run, maybe Herr Somebody had strayed from his route, the navigator fucking up over England, that was *definitely* not a friendly engine noise. And all this in no time at all, the time between grasping a glass and bringing it to my lips, carefully there to sip it, and the bartender's quizzical look, and everything rushing through this moment like dirty floodwater, and then a much worse noise, a noise worrying to the marrow of my bones, the long, mournful, excited whistle of something falling, free falling, a noise curiously like a mob of people all gabbling, and then in a spliced fragment of a second, that selfsame noise piercing through wood, no doubt the glorious roof-beams, and then – myself eternally about to drink, the corporal eternally about to speak, forever more, never leaving there again, never breaching to the next moment – a violent concatenation, the brain-melting sound of explosives catching fire, catching bloom from the devious fuze, the devious gaine, the ferocious ZUS, and taking with a great vigorous hand the entire world in its grip, the barn, the ground, the sky as far as the heavens, and wrenching everything two feet this way, two feet that way, it felt like, but the main explosion not with us, not with the corporal and me, but with my young officers and my blessed sapper in the next room, and I knew in there would be the total ravishment of light, the following thunder more thunderous than mere thunder to be found in mere clouds, the cudgel of heat forced down into their throats, the foul forearm of heat, whose fingers would clutch at their lungs, trying to drag them out, and then the great, fiery monster of the blast, all infinite smoke and objects turned into blades and missiles, and one man, as was discovered later, thrown out through the burst barn, and cast forty feet over the neighbouring roof, and later found dead in the fringes of a field of corn, and others so caught in the exalted murderousness of the blast that not a shard of them, not an atom of them could ever be found again, and as this was happening, in its own lunatic sequence, I saw, through what eyes I knew not, because I did not know if I was blind or seeing, a creature of fire and flame 'open' the narrow wooden door, queerly, strangely, and as it were look in, and stand in the room for a moment, like a ghost, like a person itself, with what history who knew only it was a history of death, in clothes of red and orange, and then, having peeked in at us, with all its cohorts of violence now let into our room also, withdraw itself, as if sucked back to rejoin its fellow murderers in the barn, and then the entire world, from Patagonia (which I knew) to the utmost boundaries of Ultima Thule, from the world of fire to the world of ice, shrugged, shrugged mightily, easily, vastly, and I felt that dire hand scrabbling for my lungs, but clumsily, woundingly, and in some filthy vagary of the blast, saw the corporal smeared like red butter against the wall, and then into this utterly shattered, ended world entered again another version of silence, and then just a great fog of storming dust, raging about me, gently, gently, almost, and if ten minutes later I knew my officers were killed, and my sapper viciously killed, and the corporal vilely killed, before all that I stood there, the dust falling around me like a million curtains, as if nothing had changed and everything had changed, and I was the bewildered citizen of two possible worlds, and then the whole back wall of the mess room fell down, and weird light plunged in, like a liquid, and my ears roared now, roared like the biggest storm ever seen in Sligo Bay, and bizarrely, bizarrely, there appeared to me, still that foot from my face, now as if floating, unconnected, and so pristine, untouched, immaculate, not a drop spilled, not a feather taken out of it, solid and clean in my hand, the pint of waiting beer.

❧

Pat Millane has been on my mind all night. I was drifting in and out of sleep under the mosquito net and in my half-sleep he would be there, chatting and smiling, with his Galway English and his Aran Irish. Uncanny and unsettling, but welcome, I didn't scorn to dream of him. Old comrades have odd afterlives in their living comrades' hearts. He was an ordinary sort of a fella, and yet, extraordinary too, and when that Messerschmitt blew up him and his comrades, and melded them into the blessed aether like a dozen starry angels, it erased a person that was an adornment to the species of man.

His army coffin contained mostly sandbags.

Furlough again, happily, because brother Tom had just been elected mayor of Sligo.

Myself and Tom went out for a drink. It was deeply pleasing somehow to see him in his 'heyday'. Tom has an easy-going soul, it is not difficult to love a man like that, and when he is also your brother, you can feel a lot of pride in the fact. We went to a little cramped bar we wouldn't usually frequent, just for the privacy of it. It was lovely to order the whiskies and just sit there on the stools, looking at the dirty Guinness bottles on the dusty shelves that passed for a tempting display. And the last valiant light of a late summer's evening outside – though the light itself was barred, you might think, from entering the dark, unwashed cave, where old Mr Ferriter stood stooped by his cash register.

'I was talking to Jonno Lynch the other day,' said Tom.

'That's the bowsie put the death sentence on Eneas.'

'Well, yeh,' said Tom. 'True enough. But he's a town councillor now, you know.'

'What, in your outfit?' I said.

'He's a very good organiser.'

'I'll say,' I said.

'Anyway,' said Tom, 'he comes over to me, Jonno does, and he leans in, and he says: "We're hoping for a German win." That's all he says, and he winks then. A German win – like the thing was a bloody soccer match. Then he says, "I suppose you'd be in two minds about the war now considering." "What do you mean?" I said, "If you're referring to Jack, we're all hoping he comes back safely, I am sure." "No," says Jonno, "I didn't mean Jack, I meant Eneas. I hear he's in the British army." "Well, sure," I said, "half the blessed world is in the British army. Eneas is just trying to do his bit, I am sure." "He did his fucking bit for Britain already," says Jonno. Jonno has an odd way of saying a savage thing humorously, so it takes the insult out of it. This was becoming an uncomfortable talk for me, and I was trying to find a way to get past him. "The RIC were cunts, Tom, cunts," he says, with that queer vehemence of his. I could see him regretting the swear word a little. "But we've nothing against Jack," says he, as if to mollify things, "sure everyone likes Jack." "How do you mean?" I said. "There's no harm in Jack," he says, like it was one of the sayings in the Bible. And I said, interested enough, you know, because I'd been wondering what sort of stance a fella like Jonno Lynch might take towards you, being in the army and all, "Sure," I said, "Jack's only in it to keep his wife in dresses." "Oh sure, we know that," says Jonno. And off he went then.'

'He's a bowsie,' I said again.

'He was very brave in the civil war,' said Tom, with an unexpected reverence.

Despite trying to keep ourselves out of the way nevertheless a few of Tom's cronies wandered in. Maybe he had told them to come in later, I didn't know. Only one of them I knew, McCarthy the champion road-bowler, whose father had been a commandant in the Tan war. He had a head on him like the top of a boggy hill, complete with little streams of sweat.

They talked passionately enough, full of jokes, joshing as always, but the thing I noticed was that they never referred to the war the whole night. I listened to the familiar talk, of land, and marts, and deals, and local scandals – but never the war. Of course they wouldn't have heard too much about it, the radio said nothing, the newspapers were blank. They had an idea about it no better than a child's. It was curious to be among them, Tom laughing with them, with the new salt on his talk of personal triumph. The doings of Sligo were paramount, and if ten thousand men had been fastened to the Russian earth by frost and blood, it meant nothing. The war was a word. I had come back from a word and was soon going back to it.

Jack Kirwan had brought Mai to Roscommon to convalesce with him and his new wife. She was back in Harbour House, Maggie restored to her side, and she was in excellent spirits. She was laughing and joking with me in a way that I had almost forgotten. Suddenly she was very supportive about the war.

'It's good that one of us is able to do something,' she said.

She cooked her famous shepherd's pie for us and the kitchen was spanking clean. It was a great comfort to be with her. She was still a little weak from the pleurisy, but the colour had come back into her face, and although she was drinking gin, she seemed to be going easy at it. I had been intending to present my plan to her for a visit to a drying-out hospital, but I thought she had had enough of hospitals for the moment, and anyway, everything seemed to be going well, and the Saturday morning I was there, she sailed out onto the town with Maggie, and they bought themselves new dresses. She got a Russian coat for Maggie, so she looked like a little general.

My wages were good so she could afford a few luxuries. There was a lot of hardship in the town because so many had left to work in the munitions factories in England, and more and more things were starting to be scarce, and a lot of little businesses had expired. Almost no one knew anything about the war but the effects were being felt nonetheless. It was as if they were living at the far, far edge of an explosion, so far the light of the blast could not be seen. There was nothing of the destruction, the utter cancellation of human things, cities erased, millions set a-wandering on the roads, that there was in Europe and all over the world. When I thought of the tragedy of Singapore . . . It was a different sort of distress, minor, by the by, and I thought they would all be very surprised, regretful and horrified if Hitler ever made it to Sligo. Even though I suppose I might have been angry at the ignorance of my own home town, it had an opposite effect. There was something poignant about it. With my greater knowledge, I felt responsible for their safety. Somehow or other the mechanism of neutrality was one that also engendered love.

Then it was over to the Mam's to see Ursula and give her whatever little gift I had for her. She was a child who gave good value for anything she was given, in the form of kisses. She was an affectionate, brave little child, all in all. When I left her this time, I felt just a little less that I was abandoning one of my soldiers in a battle zone. Surely everything was looking up, surely the gods were smiling on us again.

Chapter Twenty-two

I don't know what got into Tom Quaye and myself today but we spent a crazy hour swapping old army songs, 'Pack Up Your Troubles in Your Old Kit Bag', 'Tipperary', 'Do Your Balls Hang Low?' and half a dozen others. Queer how the First World War songs suited just as well in the Second, different though they were. Tom sings about as fine as Count McCormack, or maybe I only think so now because I have nothing to compare it to in this wilderness, except my own croaking.

❧

I was making my way along the poorest of roads near the Ishkuman Pass. It was all geology around me, and not for the first time it occurred to me that the crust of the earth was just a sort of grave for creation. I was driving a Willys jeep, through Pathan territory. It was early '45 and the war still raged on, but up here all was calm and emptiness. The threat of the Russians coming through the passes to get down into India had long receded. The Japanese were in Burma but the whole continent of India lay between me and that, a nightmare Tom Quaye knows so well. There were forces in the North-West Frontier because even places not under threat had to be manned. I was reading my *Bengal Lancer* and trying to keep my nose clean. Now I was heading over to one of the more remote mountain passes, because I had heard that a section of road had fallen into a ravine, and I was to go and see and make a decision about what should be done. So there was a day's driving and as I hadn't the luxury of a batman or a companion I was intending to put up my tent alone in the darkling hills, and was rather looking forward to it, as long as no one and nothing molested me in my isolation. Many miles back, I had come into a Pathan village, and bought some beautiful mulberry wine. It sat in an earthen pot beside me on the passenger seat, wedged in with books and binoculars and my rifle case. I was glad to take a swig now and then as I roared on through the dry air, creating behind me a great dragon of dust.

For an hour now I had seen not a human soul and I was blithely content with my task, enjoying immensely the painterly desolation of the landscape and the foggy effect of the wine. I was humming to myself the tune of 'When the Lights Are Low in Cairo', which I knew so well from Roseanne playing it as one of her special pieces in the dancehall. I was thinking again of her extraordinary beauty, and her present trouble. Father Gaunt had done for her rightly, stitched her up, and blackened her name. Poor Tom. There was no lid on his sorrow about Roseanne. She was out in Strandhill this very moment, I supposed, asleep or awake, in the wild wind or the sunlight, even as I drove through all this other wildness and strangeness of the Hindu Kush. How far away seemed Sligo, and yet, how near, how close, and all the spectres and the living of Sligo, those hearts and souls that once I knew.

Thinking these thoughts, I remember so clearly now coming round a rocky corner, where the mountain overhung the road with a massive shelf of granodiorite, the road cut into the rock deep enough to leave clearance at least for a modest lorry, indeed a type of road I had built myself here and there, leaving my anonymous signature on such rather humble work. I came round the corner and found the reported fault which I had been seeking to verify, the section of the road that had given way. It had quite disappeared, and there was just a long shaley slide into the ravine, a fact I could verify to my complete satisfaction, because I went straight into it in the jeep, the little car suddenly veering left, in a second, a splice of a second, and I had just time to curse the good soldiers who had spotted this thing without leaving so much as a makeshift marker for the unwary, or in my case the half-seas-over, before I began the descent into the lower valley, at first rushing along over the gravel, my only witnesses no doubt the cretaceous corals and calcified bivalves here and there multitudinous in the stones, denizens of some ancient sea-floor, with all the wild force of a roller-coaster car in a fairground, the jeep making a screaming noise quite disproportionate to the event, I was thinking, even as my brain surged with fear and shock, and I slammed my foot hard as I could to the brake, as if that would do any good, and then I was chopping through little bushes and altitude-afflicted miniature trees of some kind, the jeep mindlessly swathing and harvesting, and after three hundred feet of this I was ready for my Maker, because suddenly grew the thought that there might be a proper cliff-drop under this, which I foggily remembered from my careless survey of the land ahead. But before I could work up to a proper terror about this, the jeep lurched sideways, and began to turn over and over instead, tumbling and smashing and the engine roaring and the wheels raging, possibly because in my effort to remain in the vehicle I was now also pressing on the accelerator, and how I remained there so long I could not say, there was no strap or belt to keep me in my place, only the steel and canvas roof, and maybe I was churned about there in the space, I must have been, like a piece of rubbish caught in a whirlpool, and then bang, bang, everything stopped, sickeningly, something much stronger than gravel or bush had been encountered, and whatever it was had won the toss, and stopped us, me and the jeep, what was left of it, brutally, completely, and I am not sure if I was conscious then, but I seem to remember being ejected from the jeep skywards, a curious long moment as I made a violent and improper arc through the dry blue air of the North-West Frontier, maybe then striking the ground shoulder first, because when I came to that's how I was lying, on a broken shoulder, and not able to move an inch, not only because there was no fuel in my body to effect such a thing, but because the jeep was lying across my lower back and legs with all the insouciance and dead weight of a drunkard. I suppose I must allow that that made two of us. Then I blacked out.

After a long time of lying there, I woke. I saw the sun much lower in the sky and indeed beginning to tip the far upland with redness. I was groggy and without pain. Under my cheek was a black stone, which I assumed was the mashed-up gravel from the black phyllites that stood rather weirdly vertical against the hill. I knew somewhere below must be a river but I couldn't hear it for the perfect silence, deafening in its own way, only broken by the friendly song of birds whose names I did not know.

It was near to darkness and I knew at that time of the year the nights could be cold. I assumed I was done for. For one thing I still couldn't move my body, and certainly couldn't free myself of the jeep's lumpen weight.

Even my arms seemed to be trapped, so that really it was only my head was available for movement, just a few inches either way, and the only remotely comfortable position was on my right cheek, though the gravel was sharp. The truth was I was still quite drunk, and Bacchus my doctor. I knew that that would pass away. While I could have made a stab at naming every atom and speck of dust and rock in the valley, it struck me that I knew almost nothing of the fauna of that district, and inevitably the mind in that position wanders to the possibility of animals under cover of darkness going about their business of scavenging and killing in the quiet hills. I had seen porcupines and pheasants along the way, and I struggled to remember what danger a porcupine might pose to a human. Then my mind turned easily and naturally to the topic of snakes, but I managed to stifle that thought, by putting my trust in the fact that the snake is a private and reclusive creature in general. There was at least no danger of me stepping on anything now.

Fear filled me and then seemed to trickle away. There was a sudden clarity in being helpless. There were no plans to make, no routes to draw up, no water to find, no food to cook. Life was cancelled somehow. The burden of my life with Mai was inexplicably lifted. I was going to die. Would there be grief? I wondered would Maggie make her scoffing noise when she heard, as if something entirely unimportant had taken place. And Mai, and Mai? Even as I gazed about me, awkwardly noting the run of the rocks, and puzzling how there were limestone beds so near to granite, and wondering what slow catastrophes of millennia had produced such an absurdity, I was also inwardly trying to understand the story of my marriage. I gazed inwardly upon the spectacle of it. I looked at it and tried to sort and arrange its sequence of epochs. And a bell started to ring in me, a deep-voiced bell, tolling in me with dreadful but forensic meaning. Mai McNulty, her life erased even as she lived it, a sort of Life-in-Death and Death-in-Life – *all your fault*, tolled the bell, *all your fault*. That strange day, just before nightfall.

Are there things we do that rescind our humanity, and bring us a death before the real death?

What broke these thoughts was a sudden pain, so fierce it was like an animal separate from myself. It flared in my lower legs somewhere under the jeep, and began to seep up my body.

I must have passed out. Then I opened my eyes and began slowly to be aware of a puzzling sound. I thought it must be water, from higher up the valley, a deluge coming down after unseen rainfall. I listened and listened and thought I could hear not only the river coming but my own blood inside my skin, and I wondered was that it, was it just my own blood in my ears? For some reason it tormented me, not knowing, I supposed I was now half mad, and everything would be disproportionate now, and witless, and without explanation. Like my life, I was thinking, like my bloody life.

Then down the valley, just within my view, came a hundred goats, each one with a bell around its neck, the bells all together making a sound like a river, and in their company a goatherd, a young boy, with loose white trousers, long shift and round felt hat, and a sort of easy, heedless gait, as unbothered as the goats by the rough way. He gazed on me a few moments as his charges flooded past, then reached into the herd, and grabbed a nanny goat. Holding her by the front legs, he showed me her belly of teats, and with a gesture of his face and eyes asked me if I wanted to drink. Then he knelt closer to me, and though the goat kicked at my shoulders and head, he got a teat to my mouth, and I sucked on it with boundless gratitude.

This accident more or less saw me through to the end of the war, for I was seven months in hospital in India. In memory of my rescuer, the goatherd, I brought two Pathan dolls home to the girls, along with myself.

Chapter Twenty-three

Just now and then I seem, in my effort to form some sort of narrative, to touch accidentally on something rawer than a mere wound, it is more like a viciousness, a poisonous compound, that even to touch brings a sudden sense of illness and unhappiness – the opposite of the King's Touch. And at the very moment of touching there is caused also a sensation of deepest alarm, of approaching disaster, and even horror, no, especially horror, like any of those old, dark dreams of childhood when I was astray in the thickest, blackest woods, and something was creeping, creeping up on me. Waking from those dreams as a child I used to cry, and sometimes now writing in this minute-book I have cried, even when I have no idea why I am crying – and cried all the harder for that. I have invoked the gods of truth, and they will have their way with me.

The war ended. I was proud, more or less, to have served in the army. But pride in that 'foreign' war meant little in Ireland. Hundreds of thousands had traipsed over to England to work in the factories and tens of thousands had joined the various forces, and they certainly knew all about it. But the stay-at-homes, and those not inclined to favour any force allied with the British, remained blank on the subject, or vibrant with contempt. There wasn't a drop of petrol in Ireland, everything desirable was rationed, there was more turf dug out of the bogs than in all the millennia before it. The war had been just a kind of giant inconvenience.

But the war ended. I went home to silences, to surprise in people's faces, as if they had forgotten I was away – 'Ah, Jack, ah, Jack, how's it going? Where have you been, man?' And all the rest of the life-giving guff of bars.

The army offered me a half-colonelship if I would stay on afterwards. I was immensely pleased to be asked. But Mai couldn't face it, and I thought she had been through enough.

'I want you here,' she said. 'I want you here.'

There was chaos and confusion everywhere after the war, but at the same time, some mechanisms were freed up. Tom's marriage annulment came through at last from Rome. Roseanne had been accused of various things and now it was all done and dusted and as if the marriage had never been. I was sent out by Mam to the dreary tin hut with Father Gaunt to tell her this, one uncherishable day, and I was shocked to find she was pregnant, but not, it seemed, with any child of Tom's.

She never did have a child with Tom. When the baby was born, it was put up for adoption in England, through the order of nuns that my sister Teasy belonged to. Roseanne was committed to the Sligo asylum, and I believe she died of TB not too long afterwards. Thus closed a terrible chapter.

If you had told me, or Tom, or anyone, that lovely bright day when they were married in Dublin, that by war's end she would be in the mad house, and shortly afterwards die, I would not have believed you. No one could have imagined such a ferocious fate for that beauteous, shining girl.

A thousand mornings then in Harbour House, waking to find myself strewn somewhere like a length of deep-water seaweed, torn away from the sea-bed by a storm, parched, shaking my head at the world, feeling for bruises and cuts, recovering half-remembered insults and curses, surveying the debris of the night, thrown plates, cutlery, the Arklow teapot, the little Belleek basket, the Dresden shepherdess, pictures knocked down from the walls, cigarette stubs everywhere, my mother's doilies flung to the four corners of a room, carpets rucked against the walls, savagery ringing in my head, my own and hers, and if I peeped into our bedroom, yes, Mai there in the bed, her greying hair on the dirty pillows, and maybe Maggie tucked in beside her, where I must have put her yet again, Mai crying out for company, for comfort, terrified, so drunk she could not register her terror, only a receptacle of terror.

Maggie wanted to be an actress and it was decided she could go away to Dublin to the acting school there. Mam arranged for Ursula to go to Liverpool to train as a nurse. So we were left then on our own. More seldom and then not at all sounded the knock on the door, of brother or mother, as if the spinning top of our wretched life was throwing everyone off, try as they might to hang on. The only thing it seems that brings the same people back that were at your marriage ceremony, in such circumstances, is your funeral.

To part Mai from Maggie was not without its station of the cross. That night after Maggie had struggled away with her box and suitcase – it was 1947, the year of the great snow – across the flagstones of the station platform, tall as a heron, in her blue coat that thinned her even more than the thin person she was, with her stark black hair, Mai poisoned herself with gin in an enormous effort of extinction against herself that was the equal in size of the gigantic tonnage of snow that fell on Sligo, that fell on Ireland, that cast an uncanny stillness on everything, the muddled roofs of the town, the utilitarian roads, the fine houses along the Finisklin road, that froze the river itself.

It was no bother to her to down the two bottles of gin, she did it with almost a steady hand all through the evening and early night, not in her room as she usually did, but at the kitchen table itself, as if she had nothing to hide now, nothing at all. And when she had the bottles drunk, she must have disrobed herself in the freezing kitchen, she must have taken off every stitch of clothes, a woman in her mid-forties, with all her battle scars, and then walked out through the front door into the maze and haze of snow. And I only knew it because I was standing at the sitting-room window myself, looking out, gobsmacked by the continuing snowfall, and wondering would there ever be a cease to it, and I saw her thin figure about twenty feet from the house, and if she had walked on further I would never have seen her. And I raced through the room and out through the hall, and fairly galloped up the road, the snow treacherous under my slippers, so I might have been a citizen suddenly of Moscow, and I tore along as the snowflakes veritably whipped my face, whipped it and whipped it, and when I reached her, I called out, and asked her where she was going. And she said in her strange drunken voice, with its perfect diction, 'I am looking for the river,' and even though she had lost her course for the river because of the snow, she seemed inclined just to persevere on, so I rushed to her and lifted her into my arms, more or less scooped her into my arms, shocked, shocked, even in that queer emergency, by the terrible lightness of the woman, and she a tall person enough, and I carried her back, doing my best not to fall with her, marvelling also at the utter whiteness now in the world, not just covering everything but wiping it out, erasing it, as if all our story might be returned to a blank page, and nothing written on it, only perhaps the very first promise of our love.

And then, how could I leave her like that, bereft, confused, drinking with an even greater ferocity, like a child rubbing a drawing out with gigantic anger and extravagant impatience?

Something I nearly forgot, how could I forget it? Perhaps because it brought such strange sorrow after, such confusion. But a few months after Maggie left, she came home on the train one day and said she had managed to 'book' her mother – a strange term, as if it were an hotel – into a drying-out hospital in the midlands, a few miles from Mullingar. And whatever Maggie said to her mother, whatever good moment she found her in, asking her to go, Mai agreed, I could hardly credit it. And Pappy, rather than myself, why I am not sure, drove her over in his old jalopy, and he told me later, Mai was somewhat 'refreshed' as my father always puts it, but in high good spirits, and he said there really was a general feeling in that dilapidated motorcar that a great thing was afoot. And they put Mai 'under' in some fashion for ten days, with drugs of some kind, maybe morphine, I don't know, and after another ten days she was ferried back to me, as right as rain, as shipshape as a bloody ship.

'Mai,' I said, 'Mai,' not really knowing what to say, and with a few whiskies in me, and I must admit I had found the evenings very long and lonely without her, maybe that is a curious thing to say, 'you look like a girl – a mere girl!'

'I don't know what you mean by that, Jack,' she said, but brightly, 'I am no girl.'

The first thing she did was go down to Queenie's house, Queenie had five children of her own by now, and it had been many years since they had had much to do with one another, the two friends. But they went about that day, and had a lovely time, a lovely time, Mai told me that herself, and the very fact she was telling me something, in that fashion, simple, true and ordinary, gave me hope and joy.

So it was wretched, it was perhaps even evil and disgusting, that in the general atmosphere of drinking in the house, that is to say, my own drinking, she seemed to slip back into it, just as easy as a pivot into a pivot hole. I suppose that was a terrible and tragic thing. By Christ, it was.

God forgive me, I pray, God forgive me.

And she began to imagine that if only Maggie were

there she might make another attempt, another effort, but Maggie was not there, was she, she was gone, and would never be living at home again – never, never, never, never, never.

I couldn't see her so distraught about Maggie, I just couldn't. Even though I thought it was good for Maggie to get away. I put Harbour House on the market. There was no work worth taking in Sligo anyhow, after the war there was such a scarcity of everything, but decent work was nonexistent. The tens of thousands of people that had gone to England to do war work didn't even bother to come home, sure they couldn't, it would have been an absurdity. So maybe I thought I could do better in Dublin. Or that was what I told myself, as I sold the house for less than I had paid for it all those years before. I had told Mai my plan and she had not demurred, and this was no Malta plan, because when the day came, she got into the motorcar with perfect obedience, even haste, and had put on her best surviving coat as was her way in something she needed to make an effort for, rare as that was, and without looking back up the Finisklin Road, we set off for the new house in Dublin.

Of course there was nothing to be had of much desirability for the price of a Sligo house, so I had only managed to buy a rather mean little premises in Clontarf, but when we reached Dunseverick Road, Mai didn't seem to give the matter a first let alone a second thought, and assisted me in carrying in our goods and chattels, which I had dragged up from Sligo on a builder's trailer lashed to the back of the car. And though we never painted a wall in that house, or hardly changed a stick of furniture from the place we threw it that first afternoon – and indeed my boxes of books never were unpacked, but stood in the little hallway for five ragged years – it had the nomenclature of 'home' for Maggie then, after we fished her out of her digs in Westland Row. She had only been planning to come home for the holidays, I suppose, poor soul. The holidays. Not a very apt title for any of the days in that house, I must confess. A measure of ferocity, sickness, shouting, smashing of the last few things carried over from the distant, distant past, sometimes a clement time in between, when Mai's essential nature shone forth, and we laughed 'like drains' as she would say, and everything was sunny for a space – but there was a bend in every time-dulled spoon, and a crack in everything.

Chapter Twenty-four

Tomelty is his name, I discover, the white inspector as I was calling him, because he was back today, without his constable. I hardly knew who or what he was because he arrived in an enormous gabardine cloak and a pair of failed galoshes, which brought a great deal of muddy water into my living room. As he divested himself of his rain-gear, with a rather exasperated, almost savage movement of his arm, another few pints of rain were spewed across the floorboards. And within his covering he had been sweating copiously. I think I had heard the low grumble of his car arriving and had certainly witnessed it parking in the three inches of water that cover Mr Oko's property at present. And just as I was expecting more veiled threats and intimations of an unsettling nature, it turned out he was on something of a mercy mission – a friendly visit almost, except nothing could really persuade me that he wants to be on friendly terms with me.

'I understand that Mr Mensah was here to see you,' he said.

'Who is Mr Mensah?' I said. I knew it was a common

name in Accra, and the name of the famous singer, but I didn't remember knowing anyone of that name.

'The brother of the woman you may or may not have had dealings with. The man who may or may not have beaten up Kofi Genfi, unless it was you who did or did not beat him up.'

'Right,' I said, a little reassured that the whole dark affair was still cloaked in multiple ambiguity.

'It isn't important now,' said Tomelty, trying to squeeze some further moisture out of the bottom of his trouser legs, ruining the crease of his uniform in the process. 'It's a closed matter. But I have heard, the way that one hears things out here, that Mensah was extremely unhappy with his visit to you, I don't know if you want to throw light on that.'

'I can't,' I said. It seemed like a thousand years ago. 'I was in the throes of a little malarial attack. Tom Quaye was looking after things. I believe he sent him on his way.'

'Well, he has been going about the various drinking places he frequents, saying hard things about you, very hard things, and I don't know, the reason I'm telling you is, this Mensah character is quite a respectable man in some ways, despite his criminal record, and when I was questioning him I got the impression of quite a straight sort of character, you know, no double talk, no evasion, really rather raw in his honesty. So when a man like that is threatening to kill someone, I pay it more heed than when I hear a gangster do so, if you follow me.'

'I do.'

'So I would just keep a weather eye out for him, if I were you,' said Tomelty, not without a certain enjoyment I thought. He was warning me but he was also content to be alarming me at the same time.

'I'm sure he won't come out here again,' I said.

'No, no, he probably won't. But he is very vexed. He has had to pay out quite a bit of money to his friend, and he was expecting you to underwrite his losses, if you follow me. A floater, you know.'

'I'm sure he was,' I said, laughing, in my man-of-the-world guise that sometimes I find myself assuming.

'Well,' said Tomelty, giving himself a last shake before having to set out again and undoing all his good work, 'I am glad you are not too bothered. These chaps have long memories. Not unlike those wild boys in Ireland in the twenties. You won't catch me going home any time soon. No, sir.'

'That's sad,' I said.

He looked at me. Maybe he thought it was sad too, or maybe it annoyed him that I had commented on it. Maybe a real man of the world would just have let the comment pass. So many things said by Irish people can very profitably be just let pass, I suppose. But did I also see a little window of vulnerability open up for a moment? A shadow of doubt and pain across the eyes? A moment of darkness? Is this how my brother Eneas looks now when someone mentions the Tan war? Somewhere, even far away like this, catching him off guard, unawares? Eneas, who can't come home again either, but has crept back a couple of times and hidden in the Mam's house, not daring to go out in daylight, and my Mam wringing her hands in the kitchen, and weeping her private tears over him. Tomelty hadn't said before he was involved in the South, he had only mentioned his presence north of the border, if I wasn't mistaken in my recollection. Perhaps being near me again, the brother of an old Royal Irish Constabulary man, had betrayed him into the shadow of a confession. What strange men were about the earth, after this half century of wars. Men who once were true, and their very trueness turned into betrayal, as the pages of history turn in the wind. Men who were vicious oftentimes and ruthless, turned into heroes and patriots. And a hundred shades and mixtures of both. Perhaps he also took some strange comfort from my war service. Yes, just for a moment, I saw the casement of a tiny window of entry into Tomelty. There was something stricken and lost about him, just for a moment, just for a moment, and then it was as if he banged the casement shut again.

I didn't know what he was going to say, and maybe he

didn't either. He certainly wasn't a sentimentalist though. He was back all shipshape in a thrice, his hatches all battened.

'How's the diary going?' he said, nodding towards this table.

'Oh, Jaysus, it's . . .' I said, and was stuck somehow for the rest of the sentence.

'I'll get on,' he said. 'Don't forget, McNulty.' It struck me that when a policeman says your name it always sounds ironical. And he made a gesture with his right hand across his eyes, as if to say, keep a look-out. 'Mensah's a taxi driver. He can move about. He's angry. I tell you, half the time I'm out here, it's like I never left Ireland. Take away the heat and the fucking palm trees and the black skins and it's all just Ballymena in the rain, I tell you.'

And then he flung the cape over his head again and plunged back out into the deluge, like one enormous elephant ear.

It was only when he was gone that I thought maybe I should have thanked him, but it was too late, his car was creating two great vees of water as it surged away.

✢

Ursula. She had been going fine at the nursing, and she sent me a photo of herself in the nursing gear, at her graduation, and very impressive it was, and a great relief.

I sent her a five-pound note and apologised for not being there, as I thought I ought to have been.

In the midwinter of '52 I got a letter from her with such an amount of distress in it, urgently requesting funds. She said she had been dismissed from her nursing job, and was living in some hardship in Toxteth. Some ten days later I got another letter from her, saying things were better, which for some reason worried me even more than the first letter.

Off I went then to England to see what was up. I said nothing to Mai about my journey.

Toxteth had an Irish bleakness, with its lowering sky and sharp, bitter wind. When I got to her little house and was let in by her astonished self, it didn't take me too long to notice that she was very afraid. She looked trim and nice enough, but her eyes were bright with fear.

'How is poor Mammy?' she said.

'Much as always,' I said. 'Much as always.'

'Did she get my birthday card, do you know, Pop?'

'Oh, she got it, yes, and very glad she was to get it. Did she write and thank you?'

'No, but – that's alright.'

'She usen't to answer my letters, either, if that's any comfort, when I was away at the war.'

'She's no letter writer, Mammy,' she said.

'She used to write a good letter when she was teaching in Manchester,' I said. 'But that was a long time ago.'

I asked her then why she had been dismissed from her nursing job. She told me the truth straight off, which was always her way. She said she had been caught filching from the drugs cabinet in the hospital and had been sacked. Barbiturates, she said, which she had begun to take for her nerves. She was blushing now, into the roots of her hair. And then she said she had been very hungry, and homeless for a week or two, because she lost her place at the nurses' home. Then she said she met a nice man, and they were going to be married.

I asked her who this man was and she said he was called Patrick Pawu, and spelled the name for me, and she said he was the grandson of the Olowu of Owu, and spelled that out too, and I asked her if it was a Portuguese name, and she said no, it was Nigerian. My heart was panicking in my chest. The ghost of all the Ketchums and Reynoldses of the world hovered in the back of my head. I don't think I had at that time ever heard of such a thing in England, a white woman and a black man. Then I suddenly thought of Mai, and her affection years ago for the first Tom in Nigeria. But I wanted to shout at her – 'You will never be able to come home with such a man, and think of the children, think of the children you would have?' But thank God, thank God I did not.

'I love him, Pop,' she said, looking at me with those fearful eyes. She had her head lowered, for the axe, no doubt. She hadn't asked me to come, and now I was there, and now she would get her punishment.

It was like the angel rolling the stone away from Christ's tomb. I had been alone with this great boulder of a thing, the boulder that has blocked up so much of human history, the weight of dominion over others, of slavery. Then the angel rolled it away. I confess I was a bloody whiteman to the last second. But then, suddenly, freedom, true bloody freedom.

'I think it is wonderful news,' I said, astonished at the words in my own mouth. 'It is the best news, Ursula, the very best.'

I was light-headed with some species of joy.

'Pop,' she said, getting up, as happy as I had ever seen her, and she had been a child originally with a gift for happiness. 'I didn't write and tell you because I was afraid.'

'Well, don't be,' I said, 'there's no need.'

Then the fog of fear cleared from her eyes, and she put her face in her hands, and quietly wept. Had I never spoken gently to her before? I feared maybe not, I feared not. Had either of us really ever treated her with a proper measure of gentleness, as much as she deserved? Why should she have thought I would now? She had no example of it. I saw this, as if someone had shone a light into my vicious heart. I saw it, and could do nothing else but step forward and hold her in my arms.

———————

To remember drunkenness is so difficult because it is really a form of human absence, a maelstrom that blanks out the landscape. Maybe from the outside, looking at it . . . But how terrible it would be to pretend that I stood outside it all. I was fully involved in the battle, and every morning knew I had been mentioned in the dispatches of grace or disgrace. Grace, because sometimes, as rare as a hot Irish day, there was a kind of huge human kindness, descending on us, Mai and Jack, and for a little while we were in the same uniform, and fighting for the same powers. When Mai would say quick, unexpected, precious things, sweet nothings indeed, maybe engendered in gin, but priceless to me for all that. For you had to have some currency to keep going in the daylight hours of relative sobriety.

But the savagery, the gear of savagery. The subtle metallic click of the machinery, when the rack is brought to the starting point, and the ropes are tied to the body. The terrifying eloquence of the barely articulate drinker. Insults, that might have done as well in the form of a knife, fashioned into a great bludgeon, for fear it would not strike home. Our heads battered by a storm of words, shards of them, rocks of them, blades of them, bullets of them, bombs. The aftermath of surging hatred, the exhaustion when we lay as it might be in the sitting room, not in the chairs, but she maybe slumped against a wall, myself stretched flat on the floor. As if the house had been struck by a falling bomb, breaking everything, but failing to explode. So that something lay there also with its secret heart beating, ticking, and who knew the devious nature of those fuzes? Their numbers and solutions? – not I. Sad beyond words to think about, shameful, the shame the worst. Turning ourselves night after night into monsters, the creations of some failed Frankenstein – pitiful because so wretched, so base, so provisional, so stripped of all good things that she especially had once had in her in abundance. Myself no better, not a jot, but in my case, I have to think, starting with so much less. The two crazy devils in Dunseverick Road. Maggie grown up now, bestriding the professional stage, but affrighted in her bed, like a child electrified by a thrashing cable. The poor neighbours oftentimes banging on the walls. The thinning, wasting body of Mai. The ludicrous bloom of rude health on my face, the rotund, padded body. Nothing left at the centre but the cinder of what had been, splinters of the lost panel depicting our setting forth nearly thirty years before, in heroic guise, on this darkening journey.

'You piece of human excrement, you useless, whining, faithless man.'

Over and over and over again, there was no ending, and the beginning was lost in time.

In the morning – nothing ever mentioned. If a Sunday, I would watch her at Mass in St Fintan's, kneeling in the pew, hungrily praying, her face white and dusty from the worried over-use of her compact. The events of the night left behind, till it all started round again. What is the point in saying I hated her – as indeed I did, often and often – when running in the pith of things, like a vein of ravaged blood, was that love, always rising again, impervious to sense, killing and giving life in equal measure?

'Efforts' were made. A few gins less, a few whiskies less, and an effort made to go out to Jammet's restaurant, in whatever finery was at our disposal.

'We must make an effort, Jack,' she would say, and when she did say it, there was always a little trim of tears, a lace of them, around her voice.

Then we were bound to chart a choppy course to the Abbey Theatre, every couple of months, to gaze at our daughter in her new show. Mai stooped, old before her time, nervous, not sure of anything, least of all herself. Grudging the time in the seats, the frightening sobriety of it. She was not able really to 'see' Maggie, there was a blindness there, nothing was ever said about the performance or the play, as if being sober now had only the authority of dreams, and not ones a person could recount, or even remember.

Chapter Twenty-five

1952. I was working on a little water scheme in Collooney, of all places, the other side of the country, which
was just the way of things in those mad days, and one
evening I was late getting back. When I crept into the
kitchen to see if there was a sandwich to be had, starv-
ing from the drive home, I was there banging about in
the dark for half a minute before I realised she was sitting at the kitchen table. I put on the lamp beside the
cooker. She had her coat on, as if she was intending to
go out or had come back in from somewhere and had
not taken it off. Her brown hat was fastened to her hair
by a long silver pin of her mother's. It is curious to me
now how I knew almost everything about her, down to
the items of her jewellery. I suppose it was from watching her closely, too closely, or not closely enough, I do
not know. Anyway, there she sat, and even the new
creep of light against her right side did not make her
move. There was neither glass nor bottle near her. I
walked over to her and stood at her right elbow.

'Are you alright?' I said.

'I was just going to bed,' she said, as if it was the

most natural thing in the world for her to be sitting there, and she did it every night, sat there in her fine black coat with the Russian fox-fur on the collar, a coat now twenty years old and more – maybe thirty. Her dark eyes had something indeed of the fox about them, and her skin, although she was now fifty, was as smooth as an apple. There was something painterly about her, as if Whistler himself might have leapt forth from behind a door and begun to paint her, her profile strong, shadowed, and so deeply familiar to me. I myself was as sober as a baby also, because I knew I had a five-o'clock start the next morning, and I had an hour now at the drawing-board before I could sleep, with the measurements I had taken, with the help of a boy, from the levelling-stick to be transferred to the town map, and the pipelines to be marked out in my red pencil. I had been rather looking forward to the work, as sometimes my mother used to look forward to her ironing, or so she would say, at midnight, when all the household was asleep.

'Can I get you some cocoa?' I said, on an inspiration, thinking that's what normal people did at this time of night, more than likely.

'Cocoa, Jack?' she said. 'I don't think we have cocoa.'

'I think we have cocoa, I'm sure we do, I'm sure I saw a tin of cocoa in the cupboard.'

'That will have been there an awful long time. That was Ursula's cocoa.'

'It's made from the cocoa bean,' I said. 'That doesn't go off.'

So I made her some cocoa because she looked like a woman in need of something. There was no milk but I made it on water and put in lots of sugar. Then I put the steaming cup in front of her and she put out a gloved hand and held onto it.

'The perfect thing,' she said.

The next morning she told me she had to go to the city to see a particular doctor because she had been to see her GP in Clontarf and he had referred her. She said she would take the tram in, but I rang the relevant person in Collooney, Mr Ryan, who was the foreman for the job in hand, and said I would not be driving over that week. I put Mai in the car, it was a Ford we had in those days, one of those made in the factory in Cork. It was a fairly basic car but it did the job. It was a cold, bright February day under an enormous sky of etched-looking blue, and we drove across Clontarf and into the environs of the old city as if it were merely a pleasant jaunt, though truth to tell it had been many years since we had driven out on jaunts.

In Dublin the specialist brought her into his room

and examined her while I waited outside. After about an hour, they came back, looking curiously like a married couple themselves, and Mai was smiling at him, and chatting about Rosses Point. It turned out he had grown up there and was one of the Midletons, though that was not his second name. Then he made an appointment for her at the hospital in two weeks' time, and Mai and I drove home, again under the extraordinary benefice of that extravagant spring sky.

We were as peaceful as doves for the two weeks and I cooked hash for her, and chops, and even ran one night to a chicken boiled with cabbage, though even as I made it I was not sure it was a real dish. At any rate she ate it mercifully, and said it was the nicest way to do chicken. All this time she seemed very quiet, and if I am being truthful rather strange. As far as I could judge she was feeling some pain, but where I didn't think I could ask her. Every day she bathed in the bathroom, and then did her face and hair at her dressing table, which throughout all the wars and drinking had somehow remained intact and elegant in our bedroom. Then she would pick out her underclothes and the dress she wanted to wear that day, and one day we found the old mosquito boots in the back of a cupboard, and we laughed when she put them on. They barely fitted her on account of her ankles being rather swollen.

On the appointed day I drove her over to the hospital in Dublin, and she was prepped up by the nurses, and given some pills, and when she went into the operating theatre she was given gas, and she was back out in an hour that time as well, which took me by surprise, and it was just as well I had not acted on my plan to have a walk down towards the Liffey as far as the North Wall.

After a while she was put into bed in a ward and I was sitting there beside her until she came round, and then the surgeon, his name was Mr Blakely, obviously the Blakelys of Rosses Point, though I had never heard of them, but Sligo people can be somewhat ubiquitous, came in, having returned himself to his Donegal tweed suit and his stylish hat. He had very fine, very clean, long-fingered hands which I suppose was useful in his line of business, and he laid these now on the pillow near Mai's head. Mai was still groggy, but she came alive when she saw him, and smiled her confident, egalitarian smile that I am not sure I had seen that often since our marriage, but that I remembered very well from her university days, when she would be walking with friends along the tree-lined ways. He said he had made a thorough examination, he had opened up the area above the liver as it were, and had a good look, and he did not think there was anything for him to do beyond that, he had

had a look and then sewn her up again, and said he would certainly be prescribing a good regimen of pills for any pain that might arise in the coming times. He said he knew, because she had told him in his office the fortnight before, that she would appreciate him calling a spade a spade, and he would do so, and named the type of cancer that she had, and what she could expect, and all the while he spoke, Mai listened to him with the perfect equanimity of the battle-hardened soldier. It was as if you could not tell her anything too terrible, she was immune, or so her smile seemed to say.

He talked to her at length about diet, he said this was all the new talk now, the beneficial effects of good food, what to eat, what not to, and quizzed her about the degree of exercise she usually aimed for, and she said she liked to walk the dogs as far as Gibraltar, and when he raised an eyebrow at this, I explained it was a bathing place in Sligo, and for a moment I knew in her confusion she had forgotten we had moved to Dublin long since, and anyhow the two dogs were dead. Then he laughed, shook my hand, 'Of course,' he said, 'didn't I swim there as a boy,' and he took her right hand in both of his, clasped it briskly, and left us. A week later we were headed back to Dunseverick Road and all Mai had to show for her ordeal so far was the vivid purple scar across where her liver was, swollen and hard.

Every night for three months or so I read her

Dostoevsky – *The Idiot* was her favourite book – and *The Brothers Karamazov*, which she thought was a bit long-winded, but endured it nonetheless, and she liked the way Dostoevsky always wrote out the whole of someone's name, patronymic and all, in the Russian style. I tried to get her going at the Kipling but she thought *Kim* was strange, and *Bengal Lancer* she said was a lot of baloney. So I double-backed to Dostoevsky, then *Madame Bovary*, which she thought maybe the second best of the bunch. The trouble was she could do no drinking because the pain subsequent to drinking was too immense. She did try, but it was not a pleasant business, and the aftermath of vomiting and groaning too terrible and pitiful for her to want to repeat it. Bizarrely enough some of the colour came back into her cheeks, and she began to look very well, very thin and stylish anyhow, and she said she certainly enjoyed losing the weight. You can't lose enough weight, she said. She was able to wear dresses now that she hadn't worn since the early 1930s, but she had kept everything, because as she said that was *her* library, the long array of dresses, skirts, blouses, trousers, chemises and God knows what else, still just holding out in one of the wardrobes, though in truth sometimes musty and faded. I let the water scheme job in Sligo go to hell, and stayed at home, I even went into the bank in Clontarf and borrowed a few pounds on the security of her bracelets and necklaces. As if sensing something, or some information had drifted to him on the air, more mysterious but as reliable as Maria Sheridan's telegrams, her brother Jack arrived one day, all the way from Roscommon, and the two of them ensconced themselves in the bare and shameful sitting room, and talked themselves stupid, Jack emerging at the bell of evening, embracing me briefly in the hall, and driving off back to the West.

I was cooking then for the three of us, and indeed Mai stood in the kitchen peeling potatoes and talking about nothing, her serious face held sideways as she rushed the knife under the potato skin with deadly precision. In the nights I threw caution to the wind and lit the fire in the dank grate, although it was supposed to be July, and read the books to her by the light of the lengthened days, the new tar roads of Dublin transformed by the late sunlight, the hesitant tide between Clontarf and Bull Island flowing past limpid and deceptively still.

In due course the cancer bit deeper into her and we were obliged then to return to the hospital. She was put into another room than the one she had previously occupied, on her own, and I pillaged the city of Dublin for fashion magazines, and some of the time Mai was in a high good humour, and joked and talked just the way she had done as a student, as if I were her friend at college.

It wasn't that all the history of chaos fled away, or

seemed never to have happened. It was just a fleeting, blessèd time of grace, when by some mercy we were at our ease together in a fashion that we had not always managed while she was in her prime and health. It didn't mean that our sins were not forever on our heads, it didn't mean we were forgiven. And Mai certainly was not healed, and maybe there was no true joy in it for her, since she had her walking papers, and well she knew. But all the same I never saw any courage to match hers, even in a dying soldier. The wolf is always in the dog, and the briar in the rose, she did not suffer a sea change, she was still Mai McNulty, née Kirwan, and I was still Jack. But I still can never be ashamed that I loved her to the degree I did, nor can ever speak against that love, or pick over it for its veracity or trueness. For it was franked and stamped by the same hand that franks and stamps all human loves.

Chapter Twenty-six

At last the rains have stopped and although the mosquitoes are now in a ferment of happiness and hang about everywhere after dark like a crowd of cornerboys in Sligo, in particular in great clouds outside my mosquito net, the land is indisputably refreshed and with the soaked earth and the return of unmolested sunlight every green thing is reaching skywards and the leaves of the multitudinous palms are plumping out and widening at an absurd pace. Tom is instantly lightened by it all, as if the rain-clouds had had their origin in his own head. He has spent the whole day spring-cleaning, although there isn't really any spring here technically, banging the brush about the wooden floors, and singing through his repertoire of Ewe and English songs. He has also shaved, and has sprung from some protective place a new set of white clothes, trousers and shirt, and now he looks by some way smarter than me. Now I have reiterated to him my plan to drive him upcountry to see his wife. He hadn't said a word about it since I first mentioned it, and I thought possibly he had forgotten. But he beamed at me immediately, stood back on his heels, stood forward on the balls of his feet, and ceremoniously and wordlessly gripped and shook my hand.

I have a sense of myself returning home now. Now I can begin to imagine it, and, with the valuable currency of imagining it in my head, I will think soon about going. Packing up, and setting off. It makes me sad somehow to write this. I have an old steamer trunk I can throw a lot of things into, and I can send that home by ship. But I won't I think make the long sea voyage this time myself, I'll get a flight down to Lagos from the new airport, and see about a good flight to Europe from there. Everything is possible now that never was possible. When I think of that bus down through the Sahara. Although I will be sorry to go, the thought of travel as always fills me with strange hope. It will be a journey towards my daughters, and Maggie's two children, whom I have not yet seen, and maybe even Ursula now has a child, she seemed to hint as much nervously in her last letter. I will go and do my best, and these are the words of a man who has done his worst so often in the past. I will be a grandfather with sweets and toys, and a father, with what wise words I can muster, and not only that, first a long catalogue of apologies. I will apologise to them, I will ask them what I must do to prove my credentials, my bona fides as a father and a man. If there is a penitential time, I will live through it, penitently. I am humbled by my account of my own doings but it is to a great degree the history of a bad man. How we are to become good, to become better, must be my study and my science, to use all my skill whatsoever I possess to build bridges at last of some coherence and solidity between myself and them, if they even still wish for such a thing. I know from every word she says that Ursula at least feels that she had me to some perhaps small effect in her corner, and I take the risk of believing that she loves me. I certainly love her. And although Maggie is buried much deeper, encased in a sarcophagus of distrust and accusation, I must sit in that fire too, and see what is left when it has burned away whatever it must burn away. I know in my own private heart I love her, I revere her, as my first-born, as my vigorous child, as my daughter. Surely, surely, with my heart set on doing these things, I will be able to do them. I ask God to help me.

In the short term I will write to Mr Oko, and thank him. I will try to be gracious in departure, if nothing else. I would give the keys to Tom for him, if there were any keys, which there are not. The day that house keys are needed in Accra will be a dark day.

Now come swirling through my mind other tricky things, the current darknesses as one might call them, that prick me awake in the night, worry at me like internal mosquitoes, and only tiredness and the solace of the African moon in the window allow me to fall back down slowly into the merciful well of sleep. Maggie's husband for one thing, a man I suspect does not like me very much. Thinks of me in a humorous, superior way, and judges me deficient. With his odd green suit the colour of a billiard table, and his burning red beard, and his poetry writing, and his tumultuous drunkenness – well, I can't upbraid him for that. But nevertheless, one wishes something different for one's daughter, all told. Something nicer. His father is a fine person, though I met him only the once, a painter from Cork city, who I am told was out in 1916, but I should imagine has lived a quiet and sober life since then. I liked him enormously, and was very encouraged, but unfortunately I don't believe the son is made from the same stuff. And now there are the two babies, about whom I have the greatest curiosity, but don't know exactly what to do with that curiosity. Maggie has taken her tone from him, and gives me a rough ride whenever I see her – but maybe this is also the long legacy of her childhood. Otherwise she is shining out on the Dublin stage, and is considered a signal young talent. I just hope this husband of hers will not devour it, and her into the bargain. A man who can do no wrong in his own eyes is a dangerous creature. A man who feels no guilt is a dangerous creature. Mai, whom I have often thought of as a tigress, had guilt to beat the band. Better for her if she had felt nothing of that, but she did.

❧

The little nurse, working away in the background whenever I visited, she knew a thing or two. Her purpose she told me was to make sure Mai had what she termed softly 'a good death'. It seemed a lovely phrase. I had the sense Mai talked to her a great deal, told her many things. But if she did, it was all in confidence, and the nurse never breathed a word to me.

I brought Maggie and Ursula in when the message came that Mai might be failing.

Maggie sat on one of those hard metal chairs beside the bed, and Ursula stood on the other side, in the darkened room. Mai stretched out a hand to Maggie, and Maggie took it, and was so full of tears she couldn't speak. Then Mai turned to Ursula.

'Come here to me, Ursula,' she said, and Ursula, not with much idea how, but willing to make the attempt, stepped closer to the high bed, and leaned herself over to Mai, propped on her big white pillows. But it was clear Mai wanted her closer than that, and so Ursula awkwardly laid her breast along the coverlet, bent in a right angle, and Mai lifted her weary right arm and laid it against Ursula's cheek, and stroked it, and said:

'Ah sure, yes.'

Things she was not able to do living she seemed able to do dying.

After a little the two young women were brought out of the room by the nurse. I heard her talking to them quietly in that quiet language of nurses, out in the corridor. And then it was just me and Mai.

'Jack,' she said, 'has it all been no good? All a disaster?'

'Jesus, no,' I said.

Such are the embers of things spoken when the great conflagration of life is nearly over. Her voice was so faint I had to lean in to hear. Her breath was a little foul from her sickness and she smelled of bitter medicines. I can't say that I cared.

'You did look so handsome in your white uniform,' said the faint voice, 'in the photograph from the Straits Settlements,' she said, in the same whisper, as if that white uniform, from thirty-five years ago, explained everything.

'Well,' I said.

'Jack,' she said. 'It's so strange to be sober, day in, day out. I have too much bloody time to think. There are so many terrible things, terrible things. Why, Jack, why a life like that?'

'I don't know, Mai.'

'Do you think it is all so grievous I will never get to heaven?'

'I am sure you will get to heaven.'

'If that could just be true, and I could see my father once again. Just once and then they can drag me down to hell for all I care.'

'They'll drag you down to hell over my dead body,' I said.

She paused, and laughter rose from her sore body.

'Jack, Jack,' she said. 'I wanted to say something to the children. I wanted to make it better somehow. But then I didn't seem to have the words. I love you, Jack, I love them, I do, I really do. Useless, useless. The things we were given, and I threw them back in the face of God. Why, why? I am so sorry. Tell them I am sorry, won't you, Jack, when I am gone?'

The last phrase, 'when I am gone', uttered in a fearful whisper.

'I'm sorry too, Mai,' I said. 'No, we didn't do things as good as you'd like. But I will never not love you, never.'

'Nor I you,' she said, in an even smaller whisper, because she was near the last. 'Please pray for me.'

If I could calibrate these words to describe the nature of that whisper, so thin, so final, so like the spider's thread. And the surging waters of strange pride and love that rose in me as she spoke, the sister in the corner of the room, having come back in without me noticing, doing something with a candle, preparing for her last moments. It is not always possible I am sure for the soldiers of a marriage, the warriors, the defeated and the survivors in the one breath, to reach the final words that will maybe one day allow a modicum of solace. That the day will come when something that was said finally hits home, as if it were a tiny arrow let loose high into the aether, only dropping down many years later.

Then she was unconscious for many hours, breathing with some hardship. Then she breathed in one last time and then the engine of her breathing stopped. The nurse lit the candle, and opened the window, so that Mai's soul, she said, could fly up to heaven. Then she blew the candle out.

When I write these things down, good Lord, it hits me then. The arrow goes straight through my heart. I look up from the page and am surprised to find myself in Accra.

It used to be all just a fog of thought, an intimation. There is a lot to be said for this writing things down. The fog gets pushed away, and the truth or some semblance of it stands stark and naked, not always a comfortable matter, no. But that was the task in hand, I suppose, to try my utmost to throw a makeshift bridge towards the future, even though the ironwork and the cables fade away to nothing in the distant air.

I often think of that moment in the North African desert when the lark flew up. Viewing the bodies of my fellow soldiers, the heart breaking deep within the chest, and the eyes of the living soldiers in the back of the truck, just watching. The eyes of the men so fearful, perhaps rightly fearful for themselves, but also so anxious for justice, for explanation, for reason. But what reason is there for the general nature of things? I cannot say that I know.

Did the lark rising up mean anything in the upshot? When I began to fill this old minute-book, I don't suppose I really thought it did. Or I suppose I thought it did in a sort of vague 'poetic' way. I took it to mean something. But what did I take it to mean? I didn't know. Does wonder have any dominion over facts, in the end? I still don't know, I still don't know.

Oh but maybe I do know, maybe I do. That love rises like the lark even from the field of death.

She had such gifts, as well she knew, for the piano, for teaching, for fashion, even for the tennis court. Gifts that were put in the great jars of alcohol and suffocated, mummified. A formaldehyde poured round them. So that in the end of her story she might only have been a specimen, whose living attributes could not be made manifest. But our greatest trouble and our saving grace is that we have a soul. Time may seem like a great flood dragging with it all the debris of the past and catching you at last running through your own fields. Where there was once a great fire may seem only an ember now in the palm of your hand. But that ember is the soul and nothing on earth can rescind it.

I miss her face, its beauty, and its beauty lost.

Chapter Twenty-seven

At the funeral Queenie Moran came up to me quietly and said I had been the death of Mai Kirwan and that Mr Kirwan had been right to call me a scoundrel all those years ago. I couldn't find an answer. She said she felt she would be untrue to the memory of her friend if she didn't speak. Her words perhaps fell wide of the mark when she spoke them but now they reach me with their proper force.

When I contemplate the stations of her cross it is impossible to disagree with Queenie. Her unhappiness over having the babies I didn't understand, even though Mam tried to tell me. The loss of Grattan House was my doing. I responded to the death of Colin by moving further away, and then enlisting as soon as possible when war broke out. And when she plainly needed me the most, I returned to the war. And throughout everything, from the beginning, I was drinking, showing her what drinking was.

What was I supposed to do with myself? The day after the funeral, when I woke in the morning and went to the bathroom, I found that all the hair on the crown of my head had fallen out.

I tried to say proper things to Ursula and Maggie, but felt encumbered by silence, and that the distance between me and every other living soul was an immensity.

I couldn't be consoled myself because grief was like a putty stuffed into me. Tom tried to help me, even Ursula tried, but I was no good for anything or anyone.

Ursula certainly made an impact on old insular Dublin, walking along the streets with the grandson of the Olowu of Owu himself. It was a while since Dublin had had all the US servicemen, down for R & R during the war years – an invasion indeed. But even from this I was detached and though Tom asked me 'what was going on there?' I only nodded my head vaguely. 'He's a very nice fellow,' I said, 'he'll be good for Ursula.' 'And were you over for the wedding, Jack?' he said, amazed. 'I was not, Tom, because they were married quietly in Liverpool. Pappy was over though.' 'Pappy was over? No one tells me anything,' he said, as if almost regretting his own absence.

I was speaking words, but I was not really present. I was numb, hollowed out, the true sorrow and weeping came later, here in Accra, under the care of Tom Quaye, in the privacy of this small house.

I felt returned to the provisional man I had been the very hour before seeing Mai for the first time.

I went back to Sligo to see if I could find some peace and sanity there. My father and mother took me in gladly.

One day I went in to talk to her in her little parlour. Beside her chair were scrapbooks, maybe six of them, filled with random handbills, scraps of pictures, items from the *Sligo Champion* about the successes of Maggie as a child at the Sligo feis, whatever had caught her fancy in a long life of pasting and selecting, though it was not the original parlour of old, but a little room in the new, or not so new now, bungalow.

The glue, the brush and those scrapbooks seemed to me an occupation almost like the weaving of baskets by the lunatics at the asylum where she once worked. In addition each chair-back had an embroidered antimacassar, to protect against the hair-oil of Pappy, myself and Tom, and you couldn't sit down in the room without dislodging one of these, and her short arm would reach out, as if not in contact with any actual thought of hers, and set it straight behind you or under you.

So one day, mired in my own confusion, I came into the room, for no other reason than to get out of the little bedroom where I had been lurking, enduring the first days of being a widower. My mother was sitting there in her tight black dress, the sides somewhat worn and maybe even a little unwashed, and the knees shiny from where she had rubbed her hands while cooking the stewed mutton the night before. Indeed that odour of mutton hung about the house.

My mother was just sitting there. The room was the back end of the sitting room chopped off by a plaster wall, achieving an accidental repetition of the old parlour in John Street. So for a moment, in the clockless misery of grief, it was possible to imagine that it was only a brief while since I had gone into that vanished room to ask her how in the name of God I was to woo a great beauty like Mai Kirwan.

But, and there was a certain medicine in this for me, in that it distracted me, my mother was crying. Tears were stealing their way down her face, making rivulets through the face-powder, like those mysterious scribbles on the moon.

'Well, Mam,' I said, 'what is the matter?'

I thought she might be thinking of any number of things, her vanished son Eneas, who had not been seen in Sligo for about ten years, the continuing vexation that her blameless husband was to her, still so hale and hearty that he rode his big black bicycle all about Sligo and environs, and in his retirement had reverted to being purely a player of jigs and reels on his piccolo and his flute, the cello banished to a stooping position in the pantry – or a dozen other things that might have stymied her in her chair.

'Nothing,' she said.

'Well, Mam, it can hardly be nothing.'

'I am fine, Jack, I am fine.' She spoke with her usual patience and kindness, but then her head went down, and another thimble-worth of tears started down her cheeks.

'I think, Mam, you can tell me what it is.'

'Well,' she said, 'well, it's the Old Matter. The Old Matter.'

Well, I knew what the Old Matter was, and no mistake.

'What brings this on now, Mam?'

'Do you know,' she said. 'I do believe it is the death of Mai, if you will forgive me saying so. There she is, a young woman, fifty-one years old, her whole life lived, and yet here am I still, in this chair, in this house, in this town, and not knowing still a thing about myself, who I am or where I come from, or who my people were, or anything.'

And now the tears seemed to rise into her very throat, flooding up, from her very stomach, because she could barely speak.

'Mam, tell me everything you know, everything you remember, and let us just put our heads together on it, and see what we can do.'

'There is nothing to do. Didn't your father look through

the registers in the church at Collooney, where I'm supposed to be from, and not a sign of me there, not a sign. Not a sign of me anywhere,' she said.

'Mam, tell me the names you know. Just say it all out, the little remnants of things that you know.'

'No,' she said, 'no,' wringing her hands.

'Look it, Mam, it was all so long ago now, you were a little mite of a baby, weren't you, and the doings of grown-ups was none of your doing, that's all.'

She contemplated this for a few moments. Then she fetched out her hanky from her sleeve, and wiped at her nose with it, where a ticklish pearl of moisture had begun to hang.

'Well,' she said, slowly, gathering herself in, her two small hands placed now on her two small knees, 'of course my maiden name is Donnellan, and it was the name of my father, who was a soldier, and they brought me up as their own child, but I wasn't their own child. But the trouble is, I have no birth certificate, even now, and when I was marrying Pappy, I was supposed to have one by me, and I didn't, and it all had to be explained to the priest. That my mother, my mother – ' And now she stopped, so it might be thought she wouldn't speak again, but she did, she surged herself forward into speech, and it seemed to me I was no longer in the room, no longer even born myself, but that it was all long ago, when as a young girl, pregnant at sixteen, she had had the good fortune, for of course that was what it had been, to have young Tom McNulty stand by her, and want to marry her, ' – that my mother was a dancing woman, a dancing woman, Jack,' she said, as if something gritty had got into her mouth, 'called Lizzie Finn, and that she got herself in trouble with a man called Gibson, the son I was told of a lord, one of those Castlemaines over in Kerry, and that . . . And that the baby, the baby, me, was given away to Gibson's batman, when the mother died. And,' she added, but she didn't seem to have anything to say after the 'And'. Maybe she knew no more than that, and anyway this was more than I had ever heard her tell. Her face was so wet with tears she had ceased to bother about it.

'And were they married when they had you, Mam?' I said.

'I suppose they were not,' she said, with sudden vehemence.

'But did anyone ever *say* that to you, Mam? Did old Ma Donnellan ever say it? Did Pa Donnellan say it to the priest was marrying you and Pappy?'

'It's not a thing that people say out, Jack.'

'Why?'

'Because of the shame!'

'I suppose that is how it may have been. But, Mam, it doesn't feel like shame. I don't feel any shame about it. I feel sorry for you, Mam. I feel sorry for her too.'

'For who?' she said, incredulous. 'You don't mean that dancing woman?'

'Maybe I do,' I said.

My mother looked at me, as if she had never seen me before in her life.

I had spoken freely suddenly, about a matter that had only ever been in chains, of silence and unhappiness. It shocked me as much as it shocked my mother. Suddenly, there seemed a path forward, or a little item of light thrown out across an old darkness. I actually laughed, further confusing my poor mother. Because, in not being able to do anything about my wife's death, I felt I could do something about my mother's birth, unexpectedly – if only to strengthen her against her own self-accusation, and turn an evil story into a good one.

'We should drive over some day to Kerry and have tea with the Castlemaines, so we should, Mam.'

Again the amazed stare.

'Aren't they family?' I said.

'They threw me away,' she said, making a valiant attempt to return herself and me to a proper *ochón is ochón ó* about the matter.

'Sure didn't you find shelter with the Donnellans? And, Mam, you're an aristocrat, aren't you, an aristocrat, without all the trouble.'

'What trouble?' she said, suspiciously.

'A big mouldy house you can't heat, a great rake of

ragged acres, and, these times, bombs thrown in the door and the house burned.'

'What?' she said, as if worried for a moment about her own little bungalow.

'And, Mam, aren't you better off with us, who like you more than any ould lord or lady could?'

For the first time, in all my efforts, that seemed to find her funny bone. She started to laugh, a sound in our childhood that always signalled an end for a while to frost. That went on like a quiet bit of fiddle music for a bit, and then grew to a respectable volume, and then she let her head knock back with the force of the laughter pouring out of her.

Chapter Twenty-eight

The only thing I could think to do then was go back out to Africa. My memory of the first year after that is not very clear. I was drinking more heavily than I ever had, and God knows how my employers put up with me. Then came my little Damascene moment in '54, and I stopped drinking. But there is a thing called dry drunkenness, I found, and my head did not clear properly for a long time. And all the while, the very people I was working for seemed to have lost their grip on the world.

When I washed up on the Gold Coast during the Togo plebiscite, it wasn't that I lacked a moral view of things, I lacked a view, like a hotel-room window facing a high, blank wall.

Nevertheless, home on leave, I lingered for a few days in Dublin. I had had the inspiration that my mother's mother most likely had been a Protestant, which was why everything was so shrouded in mystery. I went over to the Church Representative Body and was told that if there had been a wedding, and the man was well-to-do, it might have taken place in Christ Church Cathedral. I went in there, spent an afternoon reading down the names in the marriage registry for the 1870s and 80s – and there it was, the miraculous fact, the marriage of Elizabeth Finn and Robert Gibson. And I carried that nugget of freedom home to my mother.

'The bad news, Mam, is that she was a Protestant. The good news is they were married.'

'Well, is this any improvement?' said my mother, but laughing. She was buoyant, radiant with legitimacy.

I went out to Glasnevin on the same leave because it was the third anniversary of Mai's death. There was no one else there at the grave. The mason had been in finally, after much correspondence on my part, and got up the stone, and carved her name onto it.

Mary (Mai) McNulty

1902–1953

It occurred to me that this name would signify nothing and no one except to someone that remembered her, and that had loved her, and so I resolved to do my utmost to remember and love her.

As I wandered back out through the iron gates who was coming in only Queenie Moran.

'Queenie,' I said, uneasily, remembering our last exchange of words, but glad also somehow that Mai had someone else to commemorate her.

'Oh, Jack,' she said. 'Jack.'

She was carrying a posy of freesias, Mai's favourite flowers. It was a little out of season for them, but I supposed Queenie would know people with a greenhouse.

'It's good to see you, Jack,' she said. 'How have you been?'

Words of no import, sometimes the most powerful kind.

It was from that moment on that I began to feel better, but also, much worse.

Back in Togoland, I struggled to believe in the work. Emmanuel Heyst was a charismatic man. In the first place, he had five native wives, each one more glisteningly beautiful than the last. He had gone to the immense trouble of building himself a swimming pool, right at the top of a hundred-foot hill, which is why I had doings with him in the first place. He liked to bring his white friends up there at sundown, in his fleet of ex-military jeeps, and drink his cocktails, his five black wives ranged decorously in their wooden chairs painted with gold, like the chairs and wives of a chieftain.

When he suggested his little scheme for bringing guns into the equation of the Togo plebiscite, he presented it more as a social than a commercial proposition. And although I made some half-hearted efforts in that direction, and perhaps a few cases were creamed off an assignment of official army rifles, I soon thought better of it. By then there was paperwork to undo me. And so it came about that the UN, in their surprisingly decent and roundabout way, eventually more or less cashiered me. But I can't really say I feel much guilt about it, considering the strange chaos of those times, a slow, rather murderous, dubious, disheartening chaos, when there were multiple factions in Togoland wanting multiple things, and even when they wanted the same thing that Britain wanted, which was for them to annexe themselves to the Gold Coast, it was not for the same reasons.

The same sort of men who bedevilled Tom Quaye, holding him and interrogating him as an agitator, also were busy there. My impression was of violence and coercion, covered over sometimes with official words and aspirations. And indeed having heard Tom talk about his suffering at the hands of the Accra police after the war, maybe this was more widespread than I knew. What we have done with the Kikuyu in Kenya over the last few years, which any old Kenyan hand might tell you about in whispers, over a few bitters in the Army and Navy Club in London, has been a dark, dark business. Inspector Tomelty I feel sure is not a stranger to these things. The tie with Britain is still tight here, and I am not entirely certain Tom may not even have recognised him from other days. Everything new contains the rotten cancer of the old here, as indeed we found ourselves in Ireland.

And I was thinking last night about poor brother Eneas, and what he might have got up to in the old RIC, when Ireland was moving towards independence, and there were efforts to stop it at all costs, and the Auxies and the Black and Tans causing mayhem, havoc, and despair all over Ireland. And Eneas always said the RIC kept out of that, but I didn't really believe him. Of course they didn't. He was a sort of crossed-out character. And I must admit it causes me extreme grief, as a one-time officer of the Empire, to feel, to sense, to intimate, that it has all come to this. An utterly decent man like Tom Quaye tortured with iron bars by creatures whose souls were left far behind them on the track of life. Tomelty mentioned Palestine, and if ever a person wanted to know where the hell the Black and Tans went to after Ireland, that's where they have their answer – the Holy Land.

Before the axe descended on me at work I was seconded temporarily to Suez.

One afternoon I found myself standing on the shore of the Small Bitter Lake. There were soldiers and officials milling about. There was a pale yellow sand under my boots, so finely ground by the sun and the wind of the infinite desert that even as the lake water sucked at it, it seemed to suck at the water. I took out my two passports, my British and my Irish.

Colonel Nasser was set to come across the desert and take back the Canal Zone, retrieving the Bitter Lakes and the waters of the canal back into the bosom of Egypt. Hundreds, thousands of Egyptian diggers had died into that ditch a hundred years before and anyhow it was only a zone, a sort of colonial scar, on the flank of Egypt. Its birds called with foreign cries and its fish dreamed of pharaohs not kings. Nasser was coming, with his modern tanks and his passionate soldiery. I was standing there, shuffling my passports. I imagined Nasser as being thorough, sudden, and brutal. He was up against an ancient force, an idea with an enormous juju attached to it, the insouciant might of the Empire, so I was sure he would know to strike with all his might. Expecting by the wildness and inspiration of his will to gain the day. There would be erasure and chaos, I felt that approaching.

I cast my British passport into the silky waters. I thought I would have a better chance of living, with the Irish one. The fact that Nasser never did come was neither here nor there.

Of course I was born British, like all my generation. British. Such a strange word. It means a hundred different things. People mean by it what they choose. It is a mysterious word. The British Isles, where do they lie, in what ocean?

I threw my British passport into the canal and I might as well have thrown the rest of me too. It wasn't just the part of me that had tried to think of myself as a gentleman that was over – a member of the professional classes, a British officer, a district officer in the British Foreign Service, a radio operator in the British Merchant Marine – it was the whole kit and caboodle that had been Jack McNulty. The passionate drinking man was gone, the husband was gone.

And then I made my way back to the Gold Coast, flying down by the beautiful network of airplanes and little airports, touching down here and there on the burning skin of central Africa – with my Irish passport. And came back to my little house in Accra, to the ministrations of Tom Quaye, and the slow intimation at work that something was wrong.

❧

This morning, in my shaving mirror, was I mistaken in thinking there was a new fuzz of hair on the top of my head? Tiny shoots of it, but definitely there? Not red, but white as the snows of Kilimanjaro?

I am back from my journey to Tom's village of Titi-kope.

I went into town to talk to Inspector Tomelty, despite my opinion of him, to tell him I was resolved now to leave Ghana. Some impulse brought me to do that. I didn't need to. I thought somehow I should, but could not pinpoint the reason.

We were in his wooden-walled office, in the extensive compound of the Ghana Police. Everything is shipshape there, the parade ground swept and the buildings painted freshly, in contrast to the cheerful dereliction of the district around it. He seemed at his ease throughout our meeting, and yet looked at me with his policeman's face, occasionally taking notes, but sparely. He was sweating marvellously in his stiff khaki shirt, although he was barely moving a muscle. I remembered him sweating under his rain-covering the second time we met. At any rate it was murderously, viciously hot, in the manner the world of Accra assumes after the rains. The air was not really breathable, it was like an audacious experiment to see how hot you could make a person before he started to die. There was a bottle of Scotch whisky on an iron table, but Tomelty made no gesture towards it. I was so deep in strange emotion that I felt all the old thirst, and a glass of that amber liquid seemed very desirable. I was in such an altered condition of being. If I had discovered that the top of my skull had been severed by a quick blow, so quick I had not felt it, and that the skull was only sitting on my brains like a hat, I wouldn't have been surprised.

I wasn't sweating like Tomelty, I was as dry as a hob. It was so odd to sit there with him, talking, as if he were the grown-up person of the two of us, the receiver of important truths. Suddenly I was saying all sorts of things I had not intended to say. Things I would have been afraid to whisper even when I was alone. I did not feel I could merely depart the country, I said. I wanted to know if some reparation could be made, and did he or the judiciary want to issue a charge against me. I spoke in detail about Togoland and confessed my part in the gunrunning. I said I thought it was an atrocious act in a time of great unrest and uncertainty, and absolutely contrary to what I should have been doing there. And did Mr Oko and the UN want to make a prosecution?

Even in the fierce heat I was shivering now. When I came in I don't believe I had intended to say anything except that I was going. But suddenly I found I needed to tell the whole story. It was dangerous, I suppose, ruinous, and I could see at the very fringes of his large impassive face a sort of smile, that I thought wasn't a smile of encouragement, but of mockery, kept well in check.

Then I said it seemed to me that the good people were taken out of the world first, as a sort of general rule of thumb. The good go first, and the just, and the bad and the unjust live long lives, and are never brought to book, in the main. This might have been a step too far for Tomelty, because as I finished my speech, he said:

'Is this something to do with what you were writing in that book?' Suddenly, suddenly, I liked him. Swift as a swift flying from the eaves, I liked him.

'Well, I don't know,' I said. 'That might be so.'

'I told you before, McNulty, you need to leave Ghana. It was the first thing I told you. You are going now, you say, and this is good. My warning to you from before still stands. You need to watch your back, McNulty. You've made enemies here. You need to get out now while the going is still good.'

Chapter Twenty-nine

Tom, who I might now call dear Tom, as I account him a true friend, the man after all who has made my sojourn here in Accra not only bearable, but at times lightened and valuable to me, it was about Tom that I was trying to tell Tomelty also, but I never got to it. I wish I knew more about the workings of the world as it pertains to emotions. I think I can safely say that I could throw a bridge across any span of river, I could work out the likely currents even in the rainy season, I would know the stresses on the metal and the stone, no bridge I put up would ever be washed away or fall under undue weight. Yet I am not sure I could say the same for my heart, or the heart of any other person. I've been caught out somehow in my ignorance, and it has shaken me, the degree of it.

We mounted the trusty Indian motorbike early on the morning of our journey. Tom sat behind me obligingly, and being bigger than me, and the seat higher, must have presented a rather looming figure as we progressed east along the Labadi Road. I had of course told Tom about Tomelty and his repeated warning, and though he seemed to treat the news lightly, nevertheless I did notice him glancing about in an unusual way as we left the house, and even now when we were perched on the motorbike I sensed he might be keeping a weather eye out. It made me nervous, and I wondered would we be followed now.

'I have no trust for Mensah,' was all Tom actually said about it.

We had a pretty good idea where we were going. Tom had drawn a rough map for me, and of course he knew the roads well, and the names of the places on the river where we were to take the local boats. Titikope was his own village, every person knows how to get to their own village.

An excitement had gripped him at the thought of the journey and its purpose. We had no idea what class of welcome we would get from his wife, though he had sent a letter to her a few days previously. I am not sure now what was even on my mind, what I thought we could achieve for him by going up. It was something to do with Mai, though, something, and nothing to do with her, too. I was very glad to get out onto the country roads, and I think it is true to say that I was curiously happy, as happy as I have ever been. I was doing something, tackling something, grasping a bull by the horns. I would be neutral to the occasion of his meeting her, or not meeting her, or whatever was going to befall him.

And yet be a catalyst I hoped of his improved situation. It seemed to me highly desirable that a rapprochement could be made, not least because I thought when I left Tom's employment would cease. But in truth I don't know now if my plans had anything of sense in them. They were merely intentions, isolated and separate, like the lovely plans of a child. And maybe the very childish audacity of my thinking contributed to the outcome. We were choosing to place ourselves in a landscape that wished to exclude Tom, and might always wish to exclude him, evermore – but we were challenging the facts. A landscape which entertained in potential any number of outcomes, romantic or terrifying, the return of Odysseus to Ithaca, or perishing in the attempt. Tom clung to my shirt resolutely, and when he wished me to take this or that turn in the dusty road, he would wave an arm either right or left ahead of my face, leaning forward as if crouching over me, and shout his instructions into the wind. I had a sense the whole way of the solidity of the man, a man whose body, though large, had elected not to take up one inch more space in the world than absolutely necessary, and was hard and trim behind me. Whereas my own vague corpulence seemed all the more untrimmed and even degenerate, plumped down in front of him.

The rains that had drenched the land and then withdrawn may have initially sent every growing thing into a frenzy, but now the heavy new growth was drooping. The land burned mightily in its accustomed furnace. The people we passed moved slowly in the heat, always turning their faces to view us, sometimes nodding a greeting like an Irish country person. My happiness had now acquired an extra dimension. I am not sure I have ever felt so at ease in the world, apart from the counterfeit ease offered by alcohol. If the tortured ruts and potholes of the road had allowed such nonchalance, I would gladly have waved gaily to every soul we passed.

After some hours of driving I stopped the motorbike, switched places and let Tom take the handlebars. He laughed and gripped them, and we hurtled away, he driving at twice the speed I had dared, oftentimes taking the route of the dry ridge of clay that the rains had created on the lower side of the road, and he had no hesitation in uttering whoops and cries when we came within a hair's breadth of a tumble, the back wheel sliding one way and the other, his large feet skiing along the ground, and then his laughter as he gained control again, and off we shot. It struck me then that he himself maybe expected nothing from the journey, nothing except these accidental pleasures of danger and daredevilry.

Soon we reached the first river station and we abandoned the Indian to the care of the ferryman there. Tom spoke to him in Ewe, no doubt telling him we would be back in due course for the machine. Everyone was at their ease, and Tom joked agreeably with the ferryman and his pretty daughters. Then we hoiked ourselves into the bare, unpainted vessel, of some ancient vintage, not a native craft as such but something rescued from the detritus of empire many decades back, and painstakingly kept caulked and fit for the river. We sat back on the wooden bench, and let the banks, with their fiery green, flow past. Two men in their fifties, dare I say two friends, or is that absurd of me and wrong? Two men laughing at nothing as nothing passed, and peering into quick-passing villages, and waving nonchalantly to women, girls and boys busy with what looked to me like nothing also on the riverbank. The bank would open for only seconds, showing these pastoral African scenes, and then be done with them, forget them, as the boat's rough engine chundered on, belching out black fumes from an oily hole just under the rudder.

Then we made a change of boat, in consideration of the fact that we had to head up a tributary of the river. Now we were seated on a much smaller craft, rough-hewn, but still along European lines. In my mind I imagined us taking ever smaller and smaller boats for smaller and smaller rivers, until we ended up in a hollowed-out canoe. As night came to the forest around us, and I began to worry about mosquitoes, the daytime sounds of monkeys and God knew what birds gave way to the different, more subtle, and now and then more raucous, open-hearted cries of night hunters, bird and beast. We were bedded down by our boatman in the narrow cabin, so that Tom and I lay side by side like a knight and his wife on a tomb, and slept, the very smoothness of the river granting me a beautiful sleep. When I woke the same unaccustomed feeling was in me, was it almost a euphoria of some kind, a signal of clear happiness again, again I thought, like the heart and body of a child, of the child I was myself in my father's house in Sligo. As if the day, the desirable day, was in front of me without fear or danger. We washed our faces in the passing stream, and the boatman, who must have sat up all night nursing his engine, gave us some fruit for breakfast that he may well have gathered as we went, I didn't know. And then we reached the halting spot on the river that would apparently have a track leading out of it, according to Tom, and after a walk of a few hours, bring us to Titikope.

Tom made his arrangements with the boatman, whether in Ewe or not I couldn't say exactly, though it sounded like a third language unknown to me, or Ewe in a new version or accent, the way the Irish language changes its sound, from Ulster, to Leinster, to Munster, to Connaught. He threw the saddlebag from the motorbike over his shoulder, with our few spare garments and other items, not least something in a small box he had purchased for his wife Miriam, he didn't say what. And we set off along the track, just wide enough for two walkers abreast, as if it were one clear line of argument made between the chaotic disputes of tree-roots and underwood.

'Not too far now, major,' he said, as we stopped in a clearing to rest about two hours up the track.

Then it happened. One moment he was scouting about for something, looking under branches, scuffing at the ground with his feet, I didn't know what he was looking for, when he stopped very still, and put his two hands to the sides of his neck, held them there in that strange position, squeezed up his eyes, let out a great groan of misery and pain, a sound that contained in it I am sure the pain of his whole existence in summary, stayed there immobile for a full thirty seconds, bent at the knees, stumbled forward, knelt a moment on his left knee like a person about to be knighted, his dusty hat falling off, and then down further he moved, so that I thought he was going to stop there, with his face six inches from the dirt, still the hands holding his neck, but him now gasping, as if breath was not available, was not coming, and with a terrified glance at me, a questioning, horrible glance, like a murdered man, he fell the full way, and his face struck the earth, with its inch of leafy dust, and he stayed there, the hands fallen now at his sides, the palms queerly twisted and upwards, as if he had folded himself in some way, as if he was about to complete some complicated task that required a low crouch, that called for it, a physical task, like the millions he had completed efficiently in his life, the loving of his wife, the digging in the army, the killing of the Japanese, the endless shunting about for work, hand to mouth, year to year, his grace and his bloody niceness, all stilled.

'Tom Quaye, Tom Quaye,' I cried, 'my friend! What is the matter?'

I looked about in surprise and fear. Had he been shot, silently, by someone? A stroke, a heart attack? Like someone felled in a battle, as if life itself were a battle, or a conglomeration of battles, and it had all added up to a blow, invisible, in its own time, keeping its own counsel till the last, a killing blow.

I was sure he was dead. I searched for his pulse, suddenly aware of the return of the noises in the glade, as if even the animals had held their breath a moment, but couldn't feel it. Then I went on up the track to find the village. I didn't know what else to do. I cantered along in my sticky clothes, and stumbled in desperation towards a huddled group of mud houses. As it happened, the only person there who spoke English was his wife, Miriam. I tried to explain who I was and what I was doing there and about the terrible thing that had happened to Tom. Her eyes widened with shock and surprise. She called some helpers to her and she and a little group of villagers came back down the track with me.

And there was Tom still, crouched like a Mussulman praying to Mecca.

Miriam seemed to hold back. She stopped and her companions stopped. I pointed out Tom to her, as if suddenly afraid she couldn't see him. I was worried I had not properly prepared her for this strange shock. Her husband, her husband, but what did I really know of her attitude to Tom? Maybe he had treated her cruelly, maybe he was a fantasist, I didn't know. Then she stepped from the shadow of the trees and came to my side and put a hand on my sleeve, gripping the loose cotton. And we went forward to Tom.

She knelt at his side and touched his head. Suddenly, even though I had known for certain he was dead, he lifted it, just as she touched him, and looked at her. He looked at her. She showed absolutely no surprise. He said something in Ewe and she answered.

They put together a rough bier and he was carried back into Titikope. I thought of what Tom had said about when he tried to come back from the war, that no matter what dust the witch doctor sprinkled on him at the edge of the village, Miriam had insisted he was dead. And that it followed a certain logic that he could never have entered his village, and resumed his life with his wife and children, unless he could show himself passing from death to life, in the plain evidence of their eyes.

They celebrated the return of Tom Quaye. Into the small hours we drank the palm wine. Next day I left Tom there in Titikope and made the long journey back on the Indian alone.

❧

It is morning, my last morning in this house. Last night I drove into Osu district one last time and asked the taxi company that has a tiny office there to come out at ten to bring me to the airport with my cases – the 'aerodrome' as the dispatcher called it. He said he would be sure and send someone.

'*Akbe*,' I said, '*akbe*. Thank you.'

All night I slept and had no dreams. I have put the Indian in Tom's shack and sent a letter to him that he can come and get it when he is fully well. I lugged the old steamer trunk out the back and left it, Kipling and Francis Thompson and the rest can stay, I'm tired of lugging them about. I scrubbed and cleaned the little house from stem to stern, so that Mr Oko would not think badly of me.

I suppose this is the last thing I will write in this minute-book. I'll stuff it in my valise now and burn it next chance I get. I'll go back to Ireland and tend as best I can to things. Somehow the last lesson of Tom Quaye is that everything is possible. A person may die and live again.

Unlike Tom though, I cannot really go home. Mai was my village and my country. Perhaps I may be a kind of exile everywhere, since I have lost her – until I see her again. Maybe then we will have a better chance of peace, and freedom.

I hear the taxi now, turning down into Oiswe Street. It's coming.

Note by Peter Oko, assistant officer, UN, Accra

The tragic abduction, disappearance, and presumed death of Mr John (Jack) Charles McNulty, formerly of the UN, and ex-major of the Royal Engineers, is noted and regretted. It is recommended that this document be NOT sent back to his relatives in Ireland with his other effects due to the confidential nature of some passages. It is therefore recommended that it be kept with his file here at the UN offices. The investigation into the circumstances of his disappearance is being currently undertaken by Inspector Louis Tomelty, trusted member of the Ghana Police Force, Head Office, Accra, to whom all inquiries may be directed hereafter.

Signed: Peter Agymah Oko, PhD (Oxon.)

Acknowledgements

I consulted many immeasurably helpful and inspiring books for the writing of this novel, among them:

That Neutral Island, by Clair Wills, Faber and Faber
UXB Malta, by S. A. M. Hudson, The History Press
Palestine Unveiled, by Douglas V. Duff, Blackie
Fighting for Britain: African Soldiers in the Second World War, by David Killingray, James Currey
Sligo, The Irish Revolution, 1912–23, by Michael Farry, Four Courts Press
Colonial Postscript, Diary of a District Officer, 1935–56, by John Morley, Radcliffe Press
Nightmare Convoy, by Paul Lund and Harry Ludlum, Foulsham
Geology of the Karakoram and Hindu Kush, edited by Susumu Matsushita and Kazuo Huzita, Kyoto University

And other material, notably an essay:

The Political Meaning of Highlife Songs in Ghana, by Sjaak van der Geest and Nimrod K. Asante-Darko, *South African Studies Review*, Vol. 25, No. 1.
The lyrics on page 65 are found in this essay, an English translation by Mr Asante-Darko of the original song in Twi, 'Nsuo beta a, mframa di kan', by the great Highlife artist E. K. Nyame.

The lyrics on page 26, from 'Ghana Freedom Highlife' by E. T. Mensah © RetroAfric, are courtesy of RetroAfric Music Publishing.

AVAILABLE FROM PENGUIN

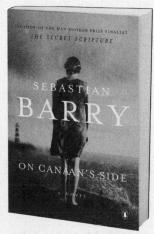

On Canaan's Side
Longlisted for the Man Booker Prize

A first-person narrative of Lilly Bere's life, *On Canaan's Side* opens as the eighty-five-year-old Irish émigré mourns the loss of her grandson, Bill, and revisits her eventful past. Forced to flee Ireland at the end of the First World War, she continues her tale in America, where she first tastes the sweetness of love and the bitterness of betrayal.

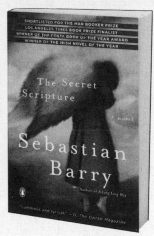

The Secret Scripture

Roseanne McNulty, once one of the most beguiling women in Sligo, is now a resident of Roscommon Regional Mental Hospital and nearing her hundredth year. Set against an Ireland besieged by conflict, *The Secret Scripture* is the engrossing tale of her life, and a vivid reminder of the stranglehold that the Catholic church had on individuals throughout much of the twentieth century.

PENGUIN
BOOKS

AVAILABLE FROM PENGUIN

A Long Long Way
Shortlisted for the Man Booker Prize

In 1914, Willie Dunne leaves behind Dublin, his family, and the girl he plans to marry in order to enlist in the Allied forces on the Western Front, where he encounters the horrors of war. Dimly aware of the political tensions that have grown in Ireland in his absence, Willie returns on leave to find a world ravaged by forces closer to home.

Annie Dunne

In 1959 in Wicklow, Ireland, Annie and her cousin Sarah live and work together on Sarah's small farm. Suddenly, Annie's young niece and nephew are left in their care. This interruption of her normal life is Annie's last chance at happiness, complicated further by the attention being paid to Sarah by a local man with his eye on the farm.

The Whereabouts of Eneas McNulty

Unable to find work in the depressed times after World War I, Eneas McNulty joins the British-led police force, the Royal Irish Constabulary—a decision that alters the course of his life. Branded a traitor by Irish nationalists and pursued by IRA hit men, Eneas is forced to flee his homeland, his family, and the woman he loves.

PENGUIN
BOOKS